ANNIE'S ATTIC MYSTERIES®

The Legacy in the Attic

DeAnna Julie Dodson

Annie's®

AnniesMysteries.com

The Legacy in the Attic
Copyright © 2013 Annie's.

Library of Congress-in-Publication Data
The Legacy in the Attic / by DeAnna Julie Dodson
p. cm.
I. Title
                    2013906455

AnniesMysteries.com
800-282-6643
Annie's Attic Mysteries®
Series Editors: Ken and Janice Tate
Series Creator: Stenhouse & Associates, Ridgefield, Connecticut

10 11 12 13 14 | Printed in China | 9 8 7 6 5 4 3 2 1

$\sim 1 \sim$

"Grammy, do you have any English clothes?"

Annie Dawson looked up from her oatmeal cookie recipe to see her twin grandchildren, John and Joanna, looking expectantly at her.

"Do you, Grammy?" Joanna asked again, her green eyes sparkling with excitement.

"English clothes?" Annie asked. "What do you mean by English clothes?"

"We want to be like Peter and Lucy, and go through the wardrobe," John said.

Annie grinned. Since the eight-year-olds had come to stay with her for a while during the summer, Annie had been reading to them again from C.S. Lewis's *The Chronicles of Narnia*. And of course, just as she had once done herself, the twins were eager to put themselves into the stories.

Annie's mind raced back to the summers of her own youth. She had come from her native Texas to Stony Point, Maine, to visit her grandparents, Charles and Elizabeth Holden, while her parents were on mission work overseas. One of her favorite haunts then was the attic of Grey Gables, her grandparents' Victorian-era home.

My goodness, Annie thought. *It's amazing how things come full circle.* Now Annie was the grandmother, entertaining her Texan grandchildren just as Betsy once had entertained her. Now the beloved Grey Gables was Annie's home, bequeathed to her after Betsy's death.

"And do you have some Narnia clothes too?" John asked, dragging Annie back to the present. "Like a knight or a king?"

"Well, let's go see what we can find."

Using a spoon to keep her place, Annie closed her recipe book and took the twins up into the attic. There was an actual wardrobe up there, one she had played in herself as a child after her grandfather had made sure the door wouldn't accidentally lock shut with her inside. Now there were some sweaters hanging in it and a pair of ski jackets, one white and one neon green, but nothing remotely English or Narnian looking.

"How about these, Grammy?" Joanna dragged over a packing box with some shoes and purses and a couple of dresses in it. "Are these English dresses?"

"Let's see." Annie pulled out one of the dresses and draped it over a little end table. It was a beaded evening dress, most likely from the early 1920s. "This looks like it might be a little bit too old for what you want, Joanna. Maybe Lucy could wear it when she's crowned queen, but let's keep looking."

"Can I play with this purse, Grammy?"

Joanna took the flashy beaded bag out of the box, and she and Annie looked inside. It still held an old compact and a comb with the name "Bonnie" set in rhinestones. Annie smiled. She remembered the purse and that old comb from when she was a little girl. They belonged to Jenny Thornton from down the street. It seemed like Annie, Jenny, and Alice MacFarlane, still Annie's best friend, had played dress-up with that same purse and evening dress a hundred times.

Joanna tugged her sleeve. "Can I, Grammy?"

With a giggle, Annie handed her the purse. "Sure, honey, though I don't think Lucy would carry one of those either."

"I like it."

Joanna put the strap around her wrist. Then she pulled a pair of purple snakeskin pumps from the 1960s off the shelf under the window and pulled them onto her bare feet.

"What about these for the fur coats, Grammy? Peter and Lucy had on fur coats when they went to Narnia, and it was always winter and never Christmas." John pulled the ski jackets out of the wardrobe and handed the neon green one to his sister. "Do you have a sword?"

Joanna obediently put on the ski jacket, and Annie couldn't suppress a laugh at Joanna's interpretation of World War II England's little Lucy Pevensie, purple heels and all.

"Do you have a sword, Grammy?" John asked again, and Annie thought for a minute.

"I know just the thing."

Several Styrofoam floating noodles were leaning in the corner of the attic. The kids used them when they played in the ocean, and cut to size, one of them would make the perfect safe sword for her little High King Peter. Annie took one of the yellow ones, thinking John could pretend it was gold, and bopped him on the head with it to make him giggle.

"Oooh, what's this? Is it an alligator?"

John dragged out the small animal, stuffed and mounted—who knew how long ago—and Annie smiled.

"Not quite. It's a caiman. It's kind of like a little alligator."

"Can we use it for a dragon?" he asked. "We might need a dragon."

"Sure. Just don't be too rough with it. It's pretty old."

Joanna looked at the creature thoughtfully. "I think we should call it Eustace."

Annie laughed. "Eustace it is."

They found an old elf costume—a lovely bright scarlet color—that Annie thought would be easy to convert into a knight's tunic and a few other useful things, and then the three of them headed toward the stairs. Annie noticed Joanna tottering on her high heels and stopped her where she was.

"I think you need to take those off until you're all the way downstairs, honey. I don't want you to fall."

With a grin, Joanna sat on the floor and took off the heels and then stuffed them as best she could into the beaded purse. Then they all trooped downstairs. When they got back into the kitchen, Joanna yanked the shoes out of her purse.

"Oh, Grammy, I tore it!"

"Oh, honey."

Annie took the bag from her and examined the lining. There was a little rip, not more than an inch or so long, in the silk. She smiled at her granddaughter.

"Don't worry. It's just a little tear. I bet I can sew it right back up for you. How would that be?"

Joanna threw her arms around her grandmother's neck. "Thanks, Grammy."

"Now, let's get all this stuff out of here, and let me see what I can do. And you'd better take that jacket off for now. It's way too hot."

Annie emptied the purse onto the kitchen counter and then examined it again, tugging the torn edges of the silk, trying to gauge how much fabric she had to work with.

"What's this?"

She saw something behind the lining, something that crackled when she moved it. She reached one finger inside the rip and touched what felt like heavy paper. Was that just part of the lining? She felt the other side of the purse, but there was nothing crackly there. It was all on one side, and it seemed to be the size of a piece of paper folded into thirds.

Curious now, she got her delicate embroidery scissors and made the hole in the lining a bit larger.

"What is it, Grammy?" Joanna asked. John was right next to her, peering into the purse.

"I'm not sure yet. It seems like there are some papers in here. I'm going to have to cut this a little bit more to get them out."

She hated to ruin the purse, but maybe she could replace the lining later. With a few more snips of the scissors, she had the papers out. They were old and brittle, and she opened the pages carefully and laid them out on the kitchen table.

The heading on the first page read, "Last Will and Testament of Paul Maxwell Butler."

"What is it?" Joanna asked again.

"It's a will from a long time ago."

John looked over his sister's shoulder. "What's a will?"

"It's a paper somebody writes to say what they want to happen to their things when they die," Annie explained.

Joanna looked at her. "Do you have a will?"

"I do."

"What does it say?"

Annie smiled. "Mostly it says that I want your mama to have everything I have."

John considered for a moment. "Did Grandpa have a will?"

"Yes," Annie said. "He did."

"Did he give everything to Mama too?"

"No," Annie said, chuckling. "He left everything to me until I die and then to your mom after that."

"But that won't be for a long time, right?" Joanna asked.

Annie smiled into the twin pairs of anxious eyes and then hugged both children close. "I hope not for a long, long time. Now, what about this will?"

"It looks like it's hundreds of years old," John said, bouncing a little.

"Not that old," Annie told him. "It's dated January 5, 1920. But that was a pretty long time ago."

"When you were a little girl?" Joanna asked.

Annie laughed. "Not quite, honey. Not even my Gram Betsy was born until a couple of years after that. I just wonder why this will was hidden in that purse lining."

Joanna was examining the hole Annie had cut in the silk. "Do you think you can fix it, Grammy?"

Annie turned her attention back to the purse. The top of the lining where the will had been hidden had been glued down, obviously to keep the papers concealed. But why? And who was this Paul Butler? Could he have been related to Ian Butler, the mayor of Stony Point? Annie and Ian had known each other ever since she had come to Stony Point, after her grandmother had died and had left Grey Gables to her, and they had been dating fairly seriously recently. Annie certainly didn't want to meddle in anything that would threaten their romance. But if this will was connected to Ian's family in some way, she was curious to know how. If this Paul Butler was old enough to have grandsons at the time he made his will, he would have been far too old to be Ian's grandfather. Maybe he was Ian's grandfather's grandfather. Or maybe Paul Butler was from some other Butler family.

She looked over the will again, skipping to the part that dealt with bequests.

> *I give, devise and bequeath to my grandson Robert Paul Mayfield, in fee simple, all of my property which I may own at the time of my death, real, personal, and mixed, tangible and intangible, of whatsoever nature and wheresoever situated, including all property which I may acquire or be entitled to after execution of this Will, to be his absolutely, if he survives me. I have deliberately made no provision herein for the benefit of my grandson Theophilus Alexander Butler, for reasons of which he is well aware.*

Paul Butler had specifically excluded his Butler grandson from any inheritance. So if there *was* a connection, Ian's family had evidently not benefited from this will. But was this the *last* will of Paul Maxwell Butler? It seemed to be properly signed and witnessed, but had it ever been properly probated? Did some later will take its place? Or had this one been concealed to prevent such a probate?

This Theophilus Butler was specifically excluded from any inheritance in this will. Did he perhaps benefit from an earlier one? Or a later one? And who had hidden this one? It was unlikely that a man would choose to hide anything valuable in a purse lining. And whose purse was it? Why would she—

"Can we, Grammy?" her grandson asked, tugging her sleeve. "Please?"

"I'm sorry, John. What?"

"Can we play Narnia now?"

Annie grinned and put the will into her recipe drawer for safekeeping. "You know, it's such a pretty day. It seems a shame to play inside."

John frowned. "But we wanted to be Peter and Lucy."

"Uh-huh. And remember where their castle was? Cair Paravel?"

"Right on the eastern sea!" Joanna said.

"And remember how the mermaids sang to them when they and Edmund and Susan were crowned kings and queens?" The twins both nodded, eyes shining, and Annie took their hands.

"Well, King Peter and Queen Lucy, how about you both put on your bathing suits so we can go down to the eastern sea and listen for mermaids?"

While the children were hurrying to change, Annie's phone rang. She was happy to hear her daughter's voice on the other end of the line.

"LeeAnn! How was your flight?"

"Long." LeeAnn sounded tired. "The trip from Maine to Texas just seems longer and longer every time. And they had us in a holding pattern over DFW for almost an hour before we were allowed to land."

"I bet you're glad to be home. And I bet Herb is glad to see you too."

"He's got a lot on his mind these days," LeeAnn said. "I didn't want to say much in front of the kids when I was up there, but he's thinking about getting a new job."

"Oh, really?"

"He says he might even want to go into business for himself. He hasn't really decided anything for sure yet."

"Doing what?"

LeeAnn sighed. "I don't know. I think he's got it pretty good where he is. We have insurance and other benefits, and they match his contribution to his retirement fund. But he got the idea that we should be doing better. He's been checking out some other jobs and even some franchise opportunities. He's got an interview day after tomorrow."

Annie blinked. "Just like that?"

"Yeah. I *don't* know what to think, actually. It just seems like such a sudden change. I like where we are. The kids are in a great school. They love their friends and their teachers. Our church is fabulous. I don't—I don't think I'm ready to start all over."

"But Herb is?"

"I don't know. I think he likes where we are too. He thinks he ought to be making more by now, and there's just not that possibility with his company at present. And of course, there was that layoff a while back—even if the company *did* hire him back. One of his buddies started his own business and has been telling Herb how great it is. I tried to tell him stability is worth a lot more to me than him earning more money."

"But it might be a great opportunity," Annie offered. "I know it was pretty scary when your dad took over the car dealership, but we made it all right."

"Yes, and it wasn't easy either. I remember all the late nights he had to work. I would've rather had him at home with us."

"It's always a trade-off, honey. The trick is figuring out what you want most. I'm sure Herb will do only what he thinks is best for all of you."

"I suppose so."

Annie could hear the reluctance in her daughter's voice.

"Maybe he won't get any offers anyway. You know how the job market is right now. Then you won't have to worry about it."

"I guess that's always possible, Mom, but from what Herb says, he's already got a couple of places really interested. Anyway, thanks for having the kids visit. Are you sure a month isn't too long?"

"Oh, no. We'll have a wonderful time. And then maybe you and Herb will have plenty of time to figure out what you ought to do."

"I guess the timing *is* perfect. We don't want to get the kids all stirred up over what might not even happen."

Annie wished she could give her daughter a hug. "Don't waste time worrying about something that might never happen, honey. Just pray that the right doors will be opened and closed at the right time. I'm sure the two of you will make the best decision for your family."

"Thanks, Mom." The lilt in LeeAnn's voice told Annie she was smiling again. "You always make me feel better. I never realize how much I miss you until I get a chance to spend a little time up there. I enjoyed our week together."

"So did I, honey. I'll have to come down and visit you again before long."

"Oh, that would be great," LeeAnn said. "Just come sometime when it's not so hot."

"That would be perfect."

"Is that Mama?" Joanna piped, hurrying into the kitchen in her pink-ruffled one-piece. Annie handed her the phone.

While first Joanna and then John chattered with their mother, Annie took out the old will, looked through it again, and then put it back into the drawer. As soon as she got a chance, she'd have to find out more about Paul Maxwell Butler.

~ 2 ~

"Come on, Tartan! Come on!"

Ian Butler ran along the beach, grinning to see his schnauzer loping toward a gathering of seagulls along the edge of the water.

"Come here, boy."

He stopped and slapped his leg a couple of times, and Tartan ran back to him, woofing and growling as if he were a much fiercer dog. Ian laughed and patted his woolly head.

"As if you'd know what to do with one of those if you caught it."

Tartan turned his head to one side and panted at him, tongue out and smiling, making Ian laugh again.

"Come on. Maybe we'll stop and see if someone at Grey Gables has a glass of iced tea and a spare doggie treat for us."

He could see the old house already and had started to jog toward it when he heard someone call his name.

"Over here!"

Annie waved to him from farther down the beach, and he made his way to her.

"Fancy meeting you here, ma'am."

"Out for your run, I see." She looked him up and down. "The sea air is obviously good for you."

He grinned, hugged Annie, and warmly kissed her. "Sea air or fine company. I can never decide which."

"Yes, I'm sure it's the company." There was a twinkle in her green eyes. "How *is* Tartan these days anyway?"

The schnauzer barked, hearing his name, and they both laughed.

"Getting some sun?" Ian asked, and Annie nodded toward the surf.

"The twins are looking for mermaids."

"Mermaids?"

"I've been reading the Narnia books to them. Right now I believe they're High King Peter and Queen Lucy."

"Oh, yeah. I was always King Peter too. What battles I won!"

"My hero." She smiled and then shaded her eyes and squinted out at the ocean. "Not too far! John, stay close to the shore!"

"They're not likely to find mermaids close to the shore," Ian told her.

"Shh." She put one finger to her lips. "Don't tell them that."

"Mr. Ian! Mr. Ian!"

The twins raced out of the water and flung themselves at him, and he gave them both a big hug.

"How are you both today?"

"We're looking for mermaids," John said, "and Grammy's making me a tunic so I can be High King Peter!"

"Won't that be fun?" Ian got down on one knee in the sand, trying to keep Tartan from licking the children all over. "I bet your grandma will have lots of interesting things for you to do all month."

"We found a dragon in the attic," Joanna told him once

she had planted a smacking kiss on the dog's furry head. "His name is Eustace."

Ian laughed. "That's as fine a name as there is for a dragon, if you ask me. And I bet he almost deserves it."

"Would you like some coffee?" Annie put her arm through his. "We were about to go in."

"Aw, Grammy." John frowned at Ian. "Do we have to?"

"Come on now." Annie took Joanna by the hand, and they all started toward the house. "It seems to me that you were the one who had a special request for oatmeal cookies today, John. I couldn't possibly make them out here on the beach."

John whooped and ran up to the front porch.

"Take your wet things off before you do anything else, and don't leave them on the floor," Annie reminded him as he disappeared into the house. Then she urged Joanna toward the door. "You too, miss."

"How about you, sir?" Annie smiled up at Ian, her green eyes warm. "Coffee?"

He grinned at her. "It's a little warm for coffee. I don't suppose you have iced tea, do you? Or have you lived up here long enough to forget that Texan necessity?"

"Of course not! And I just happen to have some in the fridge. And some pink lemonade too. What's your pleasure, Mr. Mayor?"

"I knew I came to the right place. How about some tea? With lots of ice."

She opened the screen door. "Come on in. I'll get you some."

He pulled up the bottom of his T-shirt and wiped the

sweat from his face. "I'm really not fit to come inside, plus I have this mutt along with me." He patted Tartan's shaggy head. "And I doubt that Boots would appreciate the visit. She can be a persnickety cat. Do you think we could sit out here on the porch?"

"Oh, Boots will get over it. But sure, we can sit out here, if you'd rather. I'll be right back."

She disappeared into the house, and Ian sprawled out on the old porch swing with Tartan at his feet, panting and smiling. This was good. After all the tension of the past few weeks, the run had left him relaxed and pleasantly tired. A glass of cold tea and Annie's smile would be the perfect way to end the afternoon. He closed his eyes and didn't open them until he heard the tinkling of ice.

"Oh, thank you." He sat up and took the already-sweating glass Annie was offering him. "And thanks for letting me just drop in for a handout."

She smiled and sat beside him. "You're always welcome. How's your week been? I've been so busy with LeeAnn and the twins, you and I haven't had much time to talk."

"Ugh." He leaned his head back again. "I'm just glad it's Saturday."

"Things still ... interesting at the mill?"

He sighed. Any business had its ups and downs, but lately it seemed like running the sawmill was a lot more down than up. Ian's family had owned and operated the mill for generations. Ian and his parents, Thomas and Madeleine, owned the sawmill, but Ian had managed it for years, since his father's retirement.

"Just more of the same. Somebody took wire cutters to

about twenty feet worth of chain-link fence around one of the lots."

"Oh, no."

"Oh, yeah. I hired my cousin Tim to do millwork, and all he's done so far is clean up the damage these hoodlums have been doing." He took a deep swig of tea. "Ahhh, that's good. Anyway, it doesn't look as if anything was taken. Just more vandalism."

"Any idea who might be behind it?"

"Nope. I've talked to Reed Edwards about it, and the county police, but we're a little off the beaten track out at the mill, and the county doesn't have enough men as it is."

She considered for a minute. "Maybe Reed could give you some security tips. I mean, he's not chief of police for nothing."

"You're our resident sleuth, aren't you? Maybe I should just ask you."

"I usually only look into these things after the fact," she said with a chuckle. "Obviously, I don't know all that much about crime prevention."

He pressed the cold glass against his face. "Tim's supposed to be making the rounds out that way a couple of times a night, but I guess I can't expect him to see everything."

"How is Tim doing lately, anyway?" Annie had met Tim Butler at the Butler family reunion earlier in the summer. She asked the question with a studied nonchalance, and Ian couldn't help smiling.

"Tim is Tim. He tries hard, you know, but there always seems to be something or other that gets him messed up."

She reached over and squeezed his hand, and he looked surprised at the admiration in her eyes.

"You're a good guy, Ian. Anybody ever tell you that?"

He made his expression exaggeratedly suspicious. "Me? Ma'am, I think you've confused me with someone else."

"Nope. I'm sure it's you. I don't know how many bosses would have put up with him this long."

Ian felt his face turn a little warm, and he looked into his tea, swirling what was left of the ice against the glass. "Well, he is family. Sort of."

She lifted one eyebrow. "Sort of? What is he? Your third cousin twice removed or something?"

"Hmmm. Let me see. His grandfather's great-grandfather and my grandfather's great-grandfather were brothers. That makes him what?" He counted back. "My fifth cousin?"

"I'm not sure what that makes him," she said, "but it makes you a very kindhearted and patient man."

"Aw, Tim's not so bad. As long as I keep him away from any heavy machinery or sharp instruments, he can't really hurt anything."

Ian liked the way Annie's eyes danced when she laughed, and he made a mental note to try to get her to do it more often.

"So I guess LeeAnn got back home all right? And you're planning to—"

"Grammy! Grammy!"

They both turned to see the twins at the screen door.

"When are you coming in?"

"I'll be right there, John." Annie stood up and gave Ian an apologetic smile. "I guess I'm planning to make some oatmeal cookies. You're welcome to come in. Tartan too."

Ian chuckled to see the schnauzer was sound asleep, leg twitching, and tongue lolling. "Get up, lazybones."

He gave the dog a jostling pat on the back, and they both got to their feet.

"Thanks anyway, Annie, but I ought to get home and get cleaned up. I have a ton of paperwork to get through, and it can only be put off so long."

"All right." She turned her head a little to one side. "Are you taking us to church in the morning?"

He made a slight bow. "I'd be honored."

"Come say goodbye to Mr. Ian," Annie told the children, and they came out onto the porch.

"It's good to have you both back in Stony Point. You and your grandma are going to have a lot of fun." Ian gave them a wink, and then he leaned over and gave Annie a peck on the cheek. "See you all tomorrow."

He jogged back toward the beach, Tartan loping alongside him. When he turned to wave, Annie and Joanna waved back, smiling. John only stared after him, mouth drawn down in a puzzled frown.

⁓ 3 ⁓

A quick search of the genealogy records told Annie that Paul Maxwell Butler was Ian's grandfather's great-grandfather. That was going back quite a way, but the old man was born in 1843, and he died March 4, 1920. His grandsons were probably fathers themselves by then. But his last will—the one that had been probated, the one his executor had carried out—what had it said? Maybe the one from the purse lining was just an earlier version, even though it had been dated just two months before Paul Butler's death. But it still might have been replaced—and therefore invalidated—by a later one. No need to discuss the matter with Ian if the hidden will wasn't valid.

She was glad when the Lincoln County Courthouse came into view. It was a stately looking red-brick building topped by a white bell tower. Annie climbed the front steps, went under the arched entryway and through the front door. After a few inquiries, she found where she could request copies of probate records. The woman behind the counter was slight and fortyish with overly teased dark blond hair. Her nameplate read "Carol Burke."

"May I help you?"

Annie smiled at her. "Yes, I hope you can. I'm looking for any probate records you have for a Paul Maxwell Butler.

He died March 4, 1920. I'd particularly like to get a copy of the will, if one was filed."

"Butler?" Ms. Burke lifted one eyebrow. "One of the Stony Point Butlers?"

"Well, yes, actually. How'd you know?"

"Oh, just a guess, really. I mean, obviously there are Butlers from all over, but I know about the lighthouse out there and everything. I live in Broad Cove. The Butlers of Stony Point have been well known all around there for a long, long time."

"They certainly have. I happened to come across some old records of theirs, and I wanted to find out just how they fit into the disposition of Paul Butler's estate."

"Let me see what we have. You said the date of death was March 4, 1920?"

"Yes."

She checked something on her computer screen and then smiled. "Yes, we do have a probated will on file for a Paul Maxwell Butler, date of death March 4, 1920. If you would like a copy, fill in this request form. Once you've filled it out, return it to me with the fee. That's one dollar per page for the copies. Then I'll make the copies and give them to you."

Annie smiled. "That's it? I get them right now?"

"Right now." Ms. Burke smiled too. "You fill out that form, and we'll have you on your way in no time."

When she finally had a copy of the will in hand, Annie glanced at her watch and realized the Wiscasset trip had taken more time than she had anticipated. Tossing a quick thank-you to Ms. Burke, she fished her keys out of her purse and hurried to her car. She knew she didn't have much time before the Hook and Needle Club meeting, but she couldn't resist at least a peek.

The will that had been probated and filed with the county court was dated June 7, 1917. It looked very similar to the one that had been hidden in the lining of the purse that had been up in Annie's attic. Annie scanned it quickly until she came to the bequests.

> *I give, devise and bequeath to my grandsons, Robert Paul Mayfield and Theophilus Alexander Butler, in fee simple, an equal share of all of my property which I may own at the time of my death, real, personal, and mixed, tangible and intangible, of whatsoever nature and wheresoever situated, including all property which I may acquire or be entitled to after execution of this Will, to be theirs absolutely.*

In the will she had found, Theophilus Butler had been specifically excluded from any inheritance, and Robert Mayfield had been his grandfather's sole heir. In this one—the will that had been probated and executed—Theophilus and Robert had shared the inheritance equally. But the other will, the one excluding Theophilus, was dated January 5, 1920. It should have replaced this earlier one. And if so—if Paul Butler had disinherited his grandson Theophilus—then Ian's branch of the family never should have inherited any of Paul's property—including the sawmill and the land it stood on.

"For reasons of which he is well aware." That's what the newer will had said. *Hmmm*, Annie thought. *What might*

Theophilus have done to stir up the old man's anger, or at least, disapproval? It must have been fairly serious if he went as far as completely disinheriting his grandson. She needed to get more information. But right now, she needed to get to A Stitch in Time.

*   *   *   *

"Sorry I'm running late." Annie hurried into the needlework shop, clutching the project bag that held her yarn, crochet hook, and pattern book. "I was in Wiscasset and lost track of the time."

She sat down in the circle of chairs and pulled out her latest project, a vest for LeeAnn. It was a pretty, delicate design worked in fine, cream-color yarn and done in a lacy, open stitch that would make it cool to wear even in the Texas heat.

"Wiscasset?" Alice glanced up from her cross-stitch, a glint of humor in her bright blue eyes. "And what were you up to in Wiscasset? Another of your mysteries? Or now that you're so famous for solving cases, did the police call you in on something they're working on?"

Annie shook her head. "Very funny. Actually, I was visiting the county courthouse. I don't have the twins this morning, so I thought I'd better seize the day and get up there while I could."

"So is it?" Peggy Carson set down her seam ripper and the mismatched quilt block she was taking apart. Peggy, a waitress at The Cup & Saucer, brimmed with energy when anything out of the ordinary was afoot. "Another mystery, I mean? What is it this time?"

Kate Stevens, who worked at A Stitch in Time, the needlecraft shop where the Hook and Needle Club met, grinned. "Something out of your attic again, Annie?"

Annie shrugged, not sure how much she ought to say, at least not until she really knew whether or not this affected Ian. "I'm afraid it's not much of anything at this point. Just some papers I found up in the attic. Actually, Joanna found them. Or at least, if it weren't for her, I never would have noticed them."

"So this must be some kind of humdrum case, huh Annie?" Peggy asked. Peggy couldn't get very excited about humdrum mysteries.

"Where are John and Joanna this morning?" asked Mary Beth Brock, the owner of the shop. "I was wondering if you were going to have to miss some meetings while they're here."

"Right now, they're at Vacation Bible School, but I'm going to have to get out of here right on time so I can pick them up. I think the ladies who volunteer for those kinds of things are pretty worn out by the time it's over every day. I'd hate to make them wait around just because I was late."

Gwen Palmer smiled, her blue eyes warm. "I helped out with one of the classes for several years when my kids were around that age. I enjoyed it, but you're right. I was pretty well brain-dead by the end of the week. Keeping up with that many little ones was a challenge then. I don't know if I'd have the energy to do it now."

"I know that's right," Annie said. "The twins keep me on my toes every minute, and there are just two of them. There's a reason God gives us kids when we're young."

The ladies laughed.

Kate made a few stitches in the crocheted hat she was making and then jotted down what she had just done for the pattern she was writing. Annie looked at what she already had—a thick, knobby-looking band of delicious, deep teal.

"That's going to be gorgeous," Annie said, touching her finger to the soft wool. "It looks really warm too."

"Yeah." Kate looked at her work contemplatively. "I can't imagine anyone even wanting to *look* at something like it right now, when it's so hot, but come January, it should be very popular. And of course, I have to get the pattern done and printed up in plenty of time for people to actually make the hats in time for winter. And I have some Christmas patterns I need to get out too. I'm always working in the wrong weather for whatever I'm designing patterns for, but I guess that's the only way to do it."

"How are sales these days?" Stella Brickson asked over the steady clicking of her knitting needles, eyes sharp despite her eighty-something years. "You seem to have new patterns out all the time."

Kate beamed at her. "Things are going well. It's a miracle, but sales seem to be growing each month."

"Don't let her kid you," Mary Beth said. Her voice was stern, but there was a look of fondness in her eyes for her sole employee. "Kate has worked very hard since she started selling her own patterns. If she's making a little money, she deserves it."

"You're sweet, Mary Beth." Kate squeezed the older woman's arm. "It certainly hasn't hurt that you put them in the most prominent rack in the shop, and that you talk them up to everybody you meet."

Mary Beth shrugged. "Can I help it if they're my favorites? It doesn't exactly hurt my business either to have your patterns in the shop. So it's a win-win for us both—right?"

Kate blushed a little and nodded, still smiling. "Right."

"Just be glad you two entrepreneurs aren't having the kinds of problems our mayor is right now," Peggy said. "Somebody's really giving him a hard time."

"I guess he told you about that fence being cut," Annie said.

"Yeah. He was in The Cup & Saucer a couple of days ago. He always seems in such a good mood, I couldn't help noticing he looked a little down, so I asked him what was going on."

Mary Beth looked at Annie. "What *has* been going on?"

Annie sighed. "Poor Ian, he's really been harassed by vandals lately. Nothing really major, just little annoyances mostly, until this last incident. This time someone cut up a long stretch of fencing at the mill."

Gwen laid her knitting in her lap. "Why? What does this person want?"

"That's the difficult part," Annie said. "Right now, whoever it is seems to just want to bedevil Ian. I don't know who would though. I don't think he has an enemy in the world."

"Poor Ian," Alice said. "Maybe you should find out what's going on at the mill, Annie, instead of worrying about those papers you found in your attic."

Annie shook her head. "I don't know about that. I think

whatever's going on at the mill is a little out of my league. He's got the police looking into it. Maybe I ought to just stay out of the way."

Alice chuckled. "That would be a first."

Annie shook her head and laughed with the rest of the club.

*   *   *   *

After the Hook and Needle Club meeting ended, Annie hurried out to her car, but Alice was right behind her.

"I know you have to pick up the twins, but I just can't stand it." Alice grinned at her. "Can't you at least give me a little hint about what you found?"

Annie glanced at her watch. "OK, but I have to keep it short. And you have to swear you won't breathe a word to anyone about it. *Anyone*."

Alice held up her right hand, her eyes sparkling with intrigue. "You have my promise."

"Remember Jenny Thornton, the little girl we used to play with? She lived down the street from Gram's?"

"Yeah, sure."

"We used to play dress-up with those old clothes and things from her house, remember? I guess some of Jenny's things got left at Gram's, because Joanna found one of those old purses up in my attic. She accidentally tore the lining, and I found some papers inside."

Alice's eyebrows went up. "Anything good?"

"This is the part you have to keep to yourself until I find out more."

Alice nodded eagerly.

"Well," Annie said, "the papers were an old will from 1920. It was from a Paul Maxwell Butler, Ian's grandfather's great-grandfather."

Alice gave a low whistle. "That was a while ago."

"Tell me about it, but that's not what makes it interesting. The will I found disinherits Ian's great-grandfather. If it's genuine, that means his branch of the family shouldn't have inherited the mill or the land it's on."

"No!" Alice said. "Poor Ian. What did he say when you told him?"

"I haven't told him. That's why you really, *really* can't say anything."

Alice looked at Annie warily. "Don't you think he should know?"

Annie sighed. "Of course he should, if this will is genuine. But, Alice, I just don't know enough about it yet. He's had so much going on at the mill, I hate to add this to everything else he's dealing with. I don't want to bother him with something that might not mean anything. Please! You can't tell anyone about this."

Alice held up her hand again. "Don't worry. You have my promise. But I really think you should tell him."

"Not yet, OK?" Annie gave her a quick hug. "I'd better go get the twins. I'll see you later."

*   *   *   *

Annie managed to get to the church just in time to pick up John and Joanna. The fellowship hall was decorated to look like a farm with bales of hay and chicken wire, and even a large red butcher-paper barn on one wall. From it hung a banner that said, "Get it here! Fruit of the Spirit!"

Annie smiled to see all the children milling about with straw hats on, eagerly showing their parents what they had done with their morning as the teachers in their overalls and gingham shirts began tidying up for the next day.

"Grammy!" John ran up to her and threw his arms around her waist. "Is it lunchtime yet?"

Annie laughed. "Well, I'm glad to see you too. Where's Joanna?"

"Here I am!" Joanna hugged Annie too. "See? We're learning about the fruit of the Spirit."

She showed Annie the two pages she had colored. One was a drawing of an orange and below it was the word "joy." The other was a drawing of an apple. It was labeled "self-control."

"Those are beautiful," Annie told her, and she gave her a kiss on the forehead. "We'll put yours and John's up on the refrigerator door with the bananas and the strawberries you did yesterday."

"Here's mine," John said. "Do you like them? We're going to do two every day except only one on Friday because there are only nine."

"I love them! I think these will fit perfectly on my fridge." She took both of them by the hand. "Now tell me what else you did today."

— 4 —

Vacation Bible School week was soon over, and Annie was glad for a chance to sleep in on a Saturday morning. Of course, with the twins around, there was never much sleeping in, especially when she had promised them a special treat later in the day.

Once breakfast was over and Boots had had her morning bowl of crunchies, Annie let the twins play on the swings in the backyard while she did some chores around the house. She and the children took a quick sandwich break around noon, and then she went back to making the Narnian clothes she had started the previous weekend.

Before she realized it, it was nearly five o'clock, and Ian was at the door. He snickered at the look of surprise on her face.

"You were expecting me, right?"

She laughed sheepishly and gave him a quick peck on the lips. "Of course I was. I guess I just let the time get away. Come in and sit down for a minute and let me put up my sewing. Won't be long."

Ian followed her into the kitchen and then looked over the items spread out on the table.

"Hmmm. A beaded gown and a roll of aluminum foil and a swimming noodle and what?" He flicked one of the little bells on the scarlet costume's pointy green collar to make it jingle. "An elf costume? What exactly are you up to now?"

"Well, let me see. I'm remaking the elf costume into a tunic for High King Peter. The aluminum foil is going to cover his shield. And I'm cutting the noodle in half to make him a sword he can't hurt anything with."

Ian grinned. "Good idea. And the gown?"

"That's for Queen Lucy's coronation. Won't it be pretty?"

"Joanna will be darling in it, I'm sure. Can I help?"

Annie laughed. "Did you suddenly take up dressmaking while I wasn't looking?"

"Nope. But I bet I can cut that noodle in half for you and cover the shield in aluminum foil."

"Oh, that would be great."

The twins, both of them a little rumpled-looking from their naps, came into the kitchen just as Ian finished making two "swords" out of the noodle.

"Hey there, you two," he said. "Are you wide awake?"

"Hi, Mr. Ian." Joanna beamed at him. "Grammy said we could have pizza and then go to the carnival in Damariscotta after that. I took a nap so I won't get too tired, but John didn't sleep at all. Are you coming with us?"

"That's what I'm here for. But first, I have to challenge High King Peter to a duel." He bopped John on the head with one of the faux swords and then offered him the other. "What do you say, your majesty? Are you prepared to fight for your kingdom?"

John only shrugged, and Ian bopped him again.

"Ah ha! I see the High King of Narnia is a coward!"

Annie laughed at Ian's exaggerated Spanish accent.

"You dare not face King Miraz of Telmar!" he said, brandishing the noodle at John. "Now, surrender your crown to me, and I will let you live."

John finally laughed. "That's not what he says, Mr. Ian."

"Come on, work with me here, John." Ian drew himself up again, comically fierce. "Now, will you surrender, King Peter, or die at my feet?"

"High King Peter never gives up!"

John charged at him, flailing away with his makeshift blade until Ian sank dramatically to his knees, clutching his heart.

"Narnia—is yours forever—High King." With a loud gasp, Ian toppled onto his side and was still. John prodded him once with the noodle and then crossed his arms, satisfied.

"High King Peter the Magnificent wins again."

Ian didn't move.

"Mr. Ian?" Joanna leaned over him. "Mr. Ian?"

With a growl, Ian sprang up and grabbed her, making her shriek with laughter.

Annie laughed. "All right, all right, that's enough. The High King is victorious, the villain Miraz is vanquished, and I'm hungry. Who's ready for pizza?"

"Me! Me!" Joanna bounced up and down. "I'm hungry."

"Me too," John said, and he put the noodle-sword on the table next to the other things Annie was working on.

"All right, go on up, both of you, and wash your hands and faces, and comb your hair. I'll get all this put away, and we'll be ready to go."

With Ian helping her, Annie cleared the kitchen table and put away her Narnia projects.

"You've been a big help, Ian. Thanks." She snuggled into his arms. "And you made a great King Miraz, accent and all."

Ian chuckled. "I'm not so sure John agrees with you, but at least I got him to play with me a little. I'm still not sure if he's unhappy with me, and if he is, why."

"Don't worry, honey." Annie gave him a comforting squeeze. "He hasn't said anything to me, so I think if it's anything, it must be pretty minor. I'm sure he'll get over it. Now let's go get some pizza."

*   *   *   *

Dinner was pizza at a little mom-and-pop place in Newcastle. The owners were actually from Italy, and the pizza was authentic and delicious. After eating, they drove over to Damariscotta, to the little carnival that had been set up in an empty field off the highway. It wasn't very big, but it did have several only slightly rickety rides and a wide array of booths with games and cheap-looking stuffed animals for prizes. And of course, there was popcorn, hotdogs, funnel cakes, snow cones, and tons and tons of pink cotton candy.

John and Joanna were delighted.

They rode the Ferris wheel and the merry-go-round and a ride called "Space Race" that had little rocketlike cars that went around in a circle. The funhouse wasn't much more than a trailer that rocked cumbersomely back and forth while Annie, Ian, and the twins felt their way through almost entirely dark narrow passageways and

shrieked each time they were blasted with a jet of com-
pressed air.

They tried to win prizes by throwing plastic rings
around bottle necks and by tossing quarters onto spin-
ning plates. Ian tossed softballs into bushel baskets,
but the third of his three bounced back out, so he didn't
win anything.

"They put springs behind those baskets, you know," he
told Annie as they walked away.

Annie laughed, and Joanna tugged at her hand.

"Can you win a prize, Grammy?"

"Come on and win the little girl this great big stuffed
bear!" The spare, balding man running the dart-throwing
booth grinned at her. "Two darts for a buck, and all you have
to do is pop the balloon and hit anywhere in the little red
star underneath. Easy as pie."

Annie shook her head, still laughing. "No, I'm afraid
I'm no good at darts."

"Aww, Grammy," Joanna pleaded. "Please."

"Honey, I'm not—"

"Oh, give it a try, Annie." Ian gave the man a dollar bill
and handed her the two darts. "It'll be fun."

"All right. Waste your money if you insist."

She took one of the darts, and not bothering to aim,
flung it at the board. To her amazement, there was a bang
and one of the little red balloons burst. The dart was stick-
ing in the edge of one of the printed red stars.

"Well, look at that!" Ian stared at the dart and then back
at Annie. "You did it!"

"Grammy, you did it!" John grinned.

Joanna jumped up and down. "Are you going to get the bear? The big one?"

Annie chuckled, still amazed. "Well, I suppose I could—"

"Sorry, lady." The balding man shook his head with exaggerated sympathy. "Gotta be one-hundred percent inside the line of the star to win a prize. I'm afraid you're on the line."

There was just the slightest touch of annoyance in Ian's expression. "If you're on the line, Annie, it's not by much."

Joanna's face fell. "But, Grammy, you hit it. You hit the star."

"I'm sorry, honey." Annie gave her a little hug. "But it wasn't quite good enough."

John tugged her sleeve. "But you have another dart, Grammy. You can do it again, right?"

Annie glanced at Ian.

"I'll try, John, but that first one was just lucky." She ruffled John's hair. "I'll try my best."

Ian gave her a pat on the back. "You can do it."

Joanna was standing on her tiptoes now, hands clasped eagerly together. "Come on, Grammy. Do it again!"

"OK. Here we go."

Annie took a deep breath, and as she had before, flung the dart at the board. Once again, there was a loud pop, and she saw her dart embedded in the very center of one of the little red stars. She could only laugh and throw up her hands.

"I can't believe it. I wasn't even aiming."

Joanna hugged her around the waist. "Did you win this time? Is it OK?"

"I don't see how it could be any better than that," Ian said, and he narrowed his eyes slightly at the man inside the booth.

But the balding man didn't notice. He was too busy inspecting Annie's dart from every angle, no doubt trying to figure out how to disqualify the throw once again. But the dart was firmly in the middle of the star, not even close to the line, and the man was eventually forced to concede.

He grabbed one of the four-foot-high stuffed bears, a purple one, and held it up for the crowd. "Lookie, lookie, lookie! We have a big winner here at Stars and Darts! The little lady takes home this big, big prize, and all it took was just a flick of her wrist! Just one dollar bill, just one buck, and she wins this ee-normous stuffed bear! Two darts for a dollar, folks, and you can be a lucky winner too! Come on by! Two darts for a dollar! Two for a buck! Big, big prizes!"

Finally, grudgingly, he handed Annie the bear, but she quickly felt a little tug on the hem of her shirt.

Joanna looked up at her with big green eyes. "Do you think we could get the pink one instead of the purple one?"

Annie grinned at her and then smiled at the man inside the booth. "May we have a pink one, please?"

The man shrugged, looking faintly disgusted. "Sure, lady. Whatever."

The exchange made, Annie took a look at her prize. "Umm ... OK. Now what do I do with this monstrosity?"

Ian laughed, but Joanna bounced up and down.

"I'll hold it, Grammy! I can hold it!"

"I think you'd better wait till we get it home, sweetie. It's about as big as you, and I'm afraid you'll get it dirty dragging it around on the ground."

Ian looked over the somewhat bedraggled prize. "Hey, how about you three stay here, and I'll go put this in the car?"

"Thanks." Annie gave him the bear. "We'll be right here. And when you get back, maybe we can try that little boat ride. What do you think, kids?"

John nodded. "I want to sit in the green one. It's got a sea horse on it."

"We'll make sure." Ian winked at him and then hurried off with the bear.

Annie took the twins each by a hand, and they wandered over to watch a man trying to stand up a soft-drink bottle using a little ring on a string. When he finally did it, he leapt straight up into the air with a loud, "Yes!"

Startled and laughing, Annie flinched back from him and bumped into the person behind her.

"Oh, excuse me. I'm sorry."

"That's all right."

The woman smiled and hurried away. Annie couldn't help thinking she looked familiar, but she couldn't quite place her. *Oh well,* she thought, *maybe I'll remember later where I've met her.* She looked around and saw Ian headed toward her, and then he stopped to talk to a sandy-haired man in his forties. The men walked toward her.

"Annie, I think you remember Tim. He works at the mill for me now. I've mentioned him to you before. Tim, you remember Annie Dawson from the reunion. And these are her grandchildren, John and Joanna."

Annie smiled and offered Tim her hand. "Hello there."

She looked expectantly at the twins, and they both gave the man polite hellos.

"It's good to see you again, Annie," Tim said. "Ian doesn't say much, but I can tell from what he does say that you're a pretty special lady."

Annie felt a touch of warmth in her face, but she couldn't help feeling rather pleased too, and she smiled.

"Well, that's awfully nice of you, Tim, and nice of Ian too."

Now it was Ian's turn to look a little red. "I was just telling Tim that I was surprised to have run into him here. I didn't think you were much for this sort of thing, Tim."

Tim shrugged. "Well, you know, sometimes it's fun to just hang out. We used to go to these little carnivals when I was a kid. I noticed this one the other day, and I thought I'd just check it out."

"All by yourself?" Ian asked, and Tim grinned a little.

"Well, no, not really. I'm supposed to meet her over by the funhouse in a few minutes."

"Hey, that's great. Somebody special?"

Tim shrugged, ducking his head. "Might be. Might be. We've been going out for about six weeks now. Just kind of seeing how we do together. So far it's been great."

"Well, bring her over. We'd love to meet her."

"Uh, no, I'd better not." Tim still had his head down. "She's pretty shy and everything. You know how it is."

"That's all right." Annie patted his arm. "You can introduce her when she is ready."

Tim gave her a grateful little smile. "Thanks. I kind of hate to jinx things this early, you know?"

Ian clapped him on the shoulder. "Take your time, Tim. For now, though, you'd better get going. If you keep the lady waiting too long, there might not be anything left to jinx."

Tim turned a little red. "Yeah, I guess I'd better. Nice seeing you, Annie." He bent down a little to Joanna and John. "You kids have a good time, OK?"

Joanna gave him a solemn nod, and John shrugged.

"Yeah, OK."

Tim straightened. "Nice running into you folks. Ian, I guess I'll see you later."

"OK. You two have a good time too."

Tim waved and then headed off toward the funhouse, whistling as he walked away.

"So what do you think?" Annie nodded toward Tim, grinned, and then looked around at the ragtag little carnival. "Not much of a place to take a date, is it?"

"Hey! I thought you wanted to come here!"

Laughing, Annie took Ian's arm. "I didn't mean *me*. If he and this girl haven't been dating long, this might not have been his best choice of entertainment."

"Aw, it's fun. Aren't you having a good time?"

She hugged up to him for a moment. "Sure I am—but that's because I'm with some of my favorite people in the whole world."

"Well, there you have it. It's probably the same with her."

Annie beamed at him. "You're probably right. Um, I get the impression that Tim doesn't do a lot of dating."

Ian chuckled. "So do I. Of course, he doesn't talk about personal stuff all that much, but I know it's been at least a couple of years since he mentioned having a girlfriend."

"Never married?"

"Actually, he was. Quite a while back now. He tried to open his own business, oh, maybe ten or twelve years ago. Did car repairs, mostly minor stuff, I think. He mortgaged everything he and his wife had, and then they lost it all when the company went belly-up. What I heard at the time was that she hadn't wanted him to open a business in the first place, that she just wanted him to work a steady job. I guess the marriage couldn't weather the storm."

Annie glanced toward where she had last seen Tim. "That's a shame. Bad enough to lose your business and everything you put into it without losing your family too. Did they have kids?"

"No, no kids. Probably a good thing at that point too. Still, I feel bad for him. He hasn't had much luck."

Annie smiled. "He seems happy enough though."

"Yeah. Always a smile, that's Tim." Ian chuckled when he saw John standing there looking more than a little annoyed. "I suppose you want to know why we're standing around here and not doing anything fun. How about that boat ride now?"

They were walking past the cotton candy stand when a burly, bearded man nearly bowled them over.

"Sorry," he growled and tried to move past, but Ian stopped him.

"Hey, is that you, Cliff? It's been a while."

Ian put out his hand, but the other man only shrugged and nodded at the cotton candy he held in both hands.

"Yeah, it has. Uh, how are you, Ian?"

Ian looked a little puzzled at the man's cool reception, but he smiled anyway. "Annie, this is Cliff Bonds. He owns the land that grows most of the trees we get for the mill.

Cliff, this is Annie Dawson and her grandchildren, John and Joanna."

Bonds gave Annie a nod. "Ms. Dawson. Kids."

"Nice to meet you, Cliff. How long have you and Ian been doing business?"

"Nearly a hundred years," Bonds said. "Well, our families have, at any rate."

Ian chuckled. "Before that, his family and my family were the same family."

"Really?" Annie asked.

"Yeah. We have the same grandparents five or six generations back."

Annie smiled at Bonds. "That's very interesting. And your family has been in the timber business all that time?"

"I'm sorry, Ms. Dawson. I'd love to talk family history with you, but I really need to get going. Nice to meet you." Bonds nodded. "Ian."

Before Annie or Ian could say another word, Bonds shouldered his way past a group of teenagers and disappeared around the corner of the funnel-cake booth.

"Friendly fellow," Annie deadpanned.

Ian snorted. "Well, we've never exactly been close, but we've always had a good working relationship. Of course it hasn't helped that we've been having all kinds of stupid mix-ups with his company lately too."

"Mix-ups?" Annie lifted one eyebrow. "Like what?"

"Oh, silly things. Checks they didn't get. Orders they didn't get. Invoices we didn't get. Timber we didn't get. Like all this other stuff I've been dealing with—just nuisances mostly." Ian shook his head. "Seems to be hitting me from all sides."

She squeezed his hand. "I'm sorry, Ian. Maybe the best thing you could do right now is just forget about all that and have some fun."

He grinned. "That sounds like the best idea I've heard yet. Come on, kids, I'll race you to the boat ride!"

~ 5 ~

The sun had gone down by the time they headed back toward the car. John was wobbling a little as he walked between Annie and Ian, and Annie held his hand a little more tightly.

"Are you all right, John?"

"Yeah, sure."

Annie smiled at Ian. "I think somebody's had a long day."

Ian's eyes warmed. "Come on, sport. How about a ride home, huh?"

John nodded blearily, and Ian swung him up onto his back. "Are you going to be able to hold on OK?"

"Of course I can." John tightened his hold around Ian's neck and then nestled his head on Ian's shoulder. "I'm not sleepy."

Ian winked at Annie. "No, of course not."

Annie laughed softly and then looked down at Joanna, squeezing the hand she held. "What about you, sweetie? Are you tired?"

Mouth full of pink cotton candy, Joanna only grinned and shook her head.

Annie smiled at her and then at Ian. "That was fun."

His eyes were warm. "Yeah, it was. We ought to go to one of the big fairs sometime. Maybe we could drive up to the one in Bangor when it opens. That'll be in a couple of weeks, if I remember rightly. Maybe we could go before the twins go home."

"That would be great. Of course, in Texas, the state fair is in October. That's supposed to keep it from being in the heat of the summer." Annie laughed. "It always manages to be hot for the fair anyway."

"So, is it a pretty good fair?"

"Oh, yeah. It's really big. There's lots to see, lots to do." Annie squeezed Joanna's hand again. "Remember when that goat chased you in the petting zoo?"

"Grammy! Don't tell people about that!" Joanna gave her a pretend pout but giggled too.

"Well, it was cute," Annie assured her. "And remember how surprised you were when Big Tex started talking?"

"Big Tex?" Ian asked.

Annie nodded. "Big Tex is, or was, a fifty-something-foot-tall cowboy that has stood at the entrance to the fairgrounds for the past sixty years and welcomed people in. Unfortunately, something shorted out in his head a while back, and he went up in flames."

Ian chuckled. "Only in Texas."

"And you know what?" Joanna added in a meant-to-be-scary whisper. "All that was left of him were his arms."

"Ooooh." Ian pretended to shiver, and then he grinned. "Poor old Tex."

By then they were at the car again, and being careful not to wake him, Ian settled John into the backseat next to the oversized teddy bear and buckled him in. Annie made sure Joanna's seat belt was fastened too, and then she got into the front seat.

"Everybody ready to go home?" Ian asked once he was behind the wheel.

"I am," Joanna piped. "John should have taken a nap so he wouldn't get too tired."

"Well, it's your bedtime too, missy," Annie told her. "So when we get home, you get right in bed."

"Can I sleep with Petunia?"

"Petunia?"

"Petunia!" Joanna gave the pink bear a huge hug around the neck. "Can I sleep with her in my bed?"

Annie laughed. "Sure you can, honey."

"Petunia," Ian said, chuckling. "That's cute."

Annie beamed at him. "Thanks for taking us. I think we all had a great time."

"I'm glad we went. I needed to forget about everything at the mill for a while."

"Exactly." Still smiling, Annie closed her eyes and leaned back against the headrest. "All those problems will still be there when you go back to work on Monday. No use worrying about them when you can't do anything about them right now anyway."

The next thing she knew, they were in front of Grey Gables, and Ian was nuzzling her cheek. "Come on, sleepyhead. I can't carry all of you inside."

Annie blinked and then laughed softly. "I'm sorry. I didn't mean to fall asleep on you. I guess I wasn't very good company during the ride."

"No problem. I had a lot to think about anyway."

He helped her to her feet, and she opened the back door and carefully scooped up a sleeping

Joanna. "It'll pass," she assured him. "These things always do."

"Yeah." He picked up John, careful not to wake him. They both crept into the house and up the stairs as quietly as possible.

"Just put him in his bed," Annie whispered. "He'll be fine."

By the time Annie had settled Joanna in her own bed and gone back downstairs, Ian was back in the living room with the giant pink teddy bear.

"Can't forget Petunia, you know," he said softly. "You promised Joanna that she could sleep with her."

"I'll make sure and take her upstairs when I go."

He put the bear on the couch and took Annie into his arms. "Church in the morning?"

"Of course. We'll be ready when you get here."

"This is nice." He squeezed her a little closer. "Being a little family like this."

"It is, isn't it?" She nestled her head against his chest and then giggled when she couldn't suppress a yawn. "Sorry about that. Guess I'd better get Petunia and head off to bed myself."

"All righty." He gave her one final hug and a warm kiss. "Sweet dreams."

Arms still around each other, they walked to the porch.

"Be careful going home," she said, tilting her face up to his.

He bent down to kiss her lips this time, his arms snug and warm around her, and she closed her eyes, clinging close until he stepped back from her.

"Good night, Annie." His voice was low and meltingly sweet. "See you in the morning."

She stood there on the porch, a little misty-eyed, until he drove out of sight. Then she went inside, locked the door behind her, and carried Petunia upstairs.

*   *   *   *

The following Tuesday, with the twins going on a "museum adventure" in Portland with several of the children in their Sunday School class, Annie hurried up to Wiscasset to see if she could find out what had happened to Paul Butler's property after he died. She stopped by the probate clerk's desk to ask where she would find the recorder of deeds and smiled a little when the woman at the counter greeted her.

"Hey, I saw you at the carnival on Saturday, right?" Annie asked. "I almost knocked you down."

Carol Burke nodded, looking a little sheepish. "I thought I had seen you somewhere before, but we get a lot of people in and out of here, so I wasn't sure. Were those your grandkids with you?"

Annie nodded, smiling. "They're staying with me for a while. It wasn't really much of a carnival, but we had a good time."

Ms. Burke smiled too. "So did we. My boyfriend—" She blushed and looked down. "I had fun too. May I help you with something?"

"I was just wondering where I would go to get copies of some deeds."

Ms. Burke pointed her in the right direction, and soon

Annie had copies of the deeds for the properties from Paul Maxwell Butler's estate. The sawmill and the Butler home were deeded to his grandson Theophilus Butler, Ian's great-grandfather. Paul Butler's other grandson, Robert Mayfield, had been deeded a large tract of woodland. A little more searching showed her that this piece of land had last been deeded to a Clifton Mayfield Bonds.

"Ah-ha," she said softly as she looked the deed over. "So that's what Ian meant when he said Cliff Bonds's family and his were once the same family. Ian and Cliff have the same ancestor in Paul Butler. Now Ian has the mill and Cliff has the timberland. That seems fair enough."

A quick glance at her watch told her she was again running late for the Hook and Needle Club meeting. All the ladies greeted her when she hurried into A Stitch in Time, but Alice waved her over to where she stood by a rack of cross-stitch patterns on the far side of the shop.

"There you are, Annie. Come help me for a minute."

"Hold on, Alice. Let me just put my stuff down." She dumped her purse and her project bag into an empty chair and smiled at the group. "Sorry I'm late. Anytime the twins are off on some adventure, I have to really scramble to squeeze in as many errands as I can while they're gone. I seem to be running all the time."

Mary Beth laughed. "I'm glad you could make it at all."

"Thanks. Now I'd better see what Alice needs me for."

"It's an emergency," Gwen said with a grin. "She can't decide which pattern she wants to do next."

"That *is* an emergency," Alice insisted, a twinkle in her eye. "Hurry, Annie."

Shaking her head, Annie went over to her. "OK, what is the big dilemma?"

"You know that sort of tall, narrow space in my hall? Between the doors on the left side? I really can't decide what to put there. Do you think either of these will do?" Alice owned the carriage house that had once been a part of the Grey Gables estate.

Alice handed Annie two floral cross-stitch patterns and then lowered her voice.

"OK, spill. Have you been in Wiscasset again? Have you found out anything new?"

"Yes, I have," Annie told her. "And no, I haven't. At least nothing conclusive."

"Have you told Ian about any of this yet?"

Annie shook her head, and Alice frowned at her.

"I'll tell him," Annie insisted, her voice just above a whisper. "As soon as I find out a little more. I promise."

Alice frowned again, and then, discussing the merits of each of the patterns she was considering, the two of them went back to the circle of chairs, sat down, and took out their needlework.

"What did you decide?" Peggy asked as she threaded her needle with green for the leaf she was appliquéing.

Alice shook her head. "I'm still not sure." She glanced sideways at Annie. "Sometimes it's hard to know exactly what is best."

"Well, I think you ought to have all your facts straight before you decide." Annie gave her a serene smile. "So go home and measure that space in your hall, and then come get the pattern that fits best."

Alice chuckled. "All right, I'm convinced. I'll wait." Again she glanced at Annie. "I just don't want to wait too long."

When the meeting was over, Annie pulled Alice aside.

"I still have a little time before I have to pick up the twins. You want to help me do some research?"

Alice nodded eagerly, and they headed to the library. After some searching, Annie found the record for Robert Mayfield.

"Date of death, March 23, 1920. He was only 35." Annie frowned. "He probably didn't die of natural causes at such a young age." She read further and found the cause of death. "It was an automobile accident."

Alice shook her head. "That's too bad. Poor guy."

Annie jotted down the date in her notebook and then exhaled heavily. "Mike Malone publishes *The Point* only when there's some newsworthy local happening And the paper's been around only since the mid-1950s, when his father started it and opened the hardware store. That's far too late to have information about the Mayfield accident."

"Maybe Grace Emory would have some idea about local publications in the 1920s," Alice suggested.

She and Annie hurried over to the petite woman sitting behind the library's reference desk.

"Hi, Grace," Annie said. "Could you help us with something?"

The reference librarian smiled, blue eyes warm. "That's what I'm here for. Are you running down another mystery?"

Annie chuckled. "Trying to, but not having much luck. I'm trying to get more information about a fatal car accident in 1920."

Grace's eyebrows went up. "That was a while back."

"Right. Too far back for *The Point*," Annie said.

"Do you know if there was some kind of local newspaper back in the twenties?" Alice asked.

"There was one for a while, I believe," Grace told them. "*The Stony Point Chronicle*. I'm not sure how far back it started—after the turn of the century I'm sure, and it was only weekly. It went out of business during the Depression."

Annie sighed. "I don't suppose anyone still has copies."

"No, no copies." Grace grinned at her. "But they left behind their 'morgue'—all the files with their records and everything—when they went out of business. When the building was sold years later, the new owner found it all and donated it to the library. We had it microfilmed."

"Oh, Grace, that's amazing! Could we look at those?"

Annie couldn't hide the smile that was plastered on her face as she and Alice followed Grace back to the microfilm reader. In a few minutes, they were looking at white-on-black reversed images of *The Stony Point Chronicle*.

Annie scanned through the headlines, lingering briefly over a few.

"I could lose myself in these old papers." She sighed. "There's something so tangible and immediate about them."

Alice nodded. "I know. Reading from history books— even the history of Stony Point—is so much more ... well, detached."

Once Annie reached March 1920, she looked at the dates more closely. March 31. March 24. She stopped there.

"I guess with so prominent a local family, the accident was front-page news."

LOCAL COUPLE KILLED IN AUTOMOBILE CRASH

In a tragic accident, Stony Point resident Robert Paul Mayfield, 35, and his wife, Bonnie Marie Mayfield, 33, were killed when Mr. Mayfield's Oldsmobile touring car veered off Ocean Drive Tuesday night at about six in the evening and crashed into a stand of trees. No other vehicles were involved.

Although there were no witnesses to the accident itself, Minnie Clifton, who waited on the couple at the Riverside Café in Newcastle, claimed that they seemed to be quarreling, but the subject of the quarrel was unclear. She could not say whether recent concerns Mr. Mayfield made public in this newspaper might have been the topic of discussion.

Police have found no direct cause of the accident, but presently assume that, distracted by this quarrel, Mr. Mayfield lost control of the car and struck the trees.

The Mayfields are survived by their nine-year-old daughter, Miss Caroline Ann Mayfield; Mrs. Mayfield's parents, Mr. and Mrs. James Thornton; and her brother, Ralph Thornton, all of No. 6 Ocean Drive in Stony Point. Funeral services for the couple will be held on Thursday at 2 o'clock in the afternoon at Stony Point Community Church.

Annie blinked. "No. 6 Ocean Drive? The house down the street from Grey Gables? Where the Chapmans live now? Bonnie Mayfield's parents lived there?" Annie shook her head. "That must mean Jenny Thornton was related to the Mayfields."

"That makes sense," Alice said. "And the Mayfields' accident had happened on Ocean Drive. Do you think they were headed to visit Bonnie Mayfield's parents?"

Annie glanced at the article again. "They had been in Newcastle for dinner, so they wouldn't have been going to their house to eat. But the article mentions the Mayfields had a daughter. How old did the article say she was at the time of the accident?"

"Nine," Alice said. "Maybe she had been staying with her grandparents while her mother and father went out."

That made sense. Annie looked over the article again. *She could not say whether recent concerns Mr. Mayfield made public in this newspaper might have been the topic of discussion.*

"Did you notice this part, Alice?" Annie pointed to the screen. "What 'recent concerns' might Robert Mayfield have had? And why would he have made them public?"

"Yeah, and in print?" Alice chuckled. "In 1920, that would have been a local scandal in and of itself."

Annie scanned through some of the newspapers dating from before the accident. An article dated March 17, 1920, caught her eye.

BUTLER HEIRS DISPUTE

The recent death of Paul Butler, the owner of Butler's Sawmill, has stirred up an unexpected controversy. When he passed away on the 4th of this month, the cause of death was reported to be heart failure, something not unexpected in a man of 76 years of age. However Robert Mayfield, the decedent's grandson and heir to half of his estate, has publicly expressed dissatisfaction with that conclusion.

"Grandfather was in excellent health; I don't

care how old he was. I visited with him the evening
he died, and he was in good spirits and feeling quite
well. I cannot believe that, due to any natural cause,
he would have passed away only hours later."

When asked to elaborate, Mr. Mayfield seemed
reluctant to give any specifics.

"I'm not accusing anyone of anything at this
point. I just want the coroner and other local au-
thorities to investigate the irregularities of this case."

Despite the objections of other family members,
Mr. Mayfield obtained a court order to have his grandfather's body exhumed and re-examined. Dr. C.S.
Maida, Mr. Butler's physician, has since confirmed the
original cause of death, and this finding has been cor-
roborated by the local coroner's office.

Theo Butler, Mayfield's cousin and co-heir, and
declined comment.

Annie sat for a moment, staring at the article. Finally,
Alice nudged her. "What?"

Annie shrugged. "The will I found disinherited this Theo
Butler—Theophilus was his given name—'for reasons of
which he is well aware.' I wonder what those reasons were?"

Frowning, Alice shook her head. "At this point, is there
any way of finding out?"

Annie pursed her lips. "Maybe there's a relative of Ian's
who kept up with old letters or journals or even stories
about the family."

"If there is," Alice said, "the only way you'll be able to
find out about it is to tell Ian what you've found out so far."

Pretending she hadn't noticed the disapproval on Alice's face, Annie turned back to the microfilm reader and scanned through a few more newspapers until she found an obituary in the March 10 edition of the *Chronicle*.

> *BUTLER, PAUL MAXWELL*
>
> *Mr. Paul Maxwell Butler passed away suddenly at his home Thursday, March 4, 1920, at age 76.*
>
> *Mr. Butler was born in Stony Point on June 22, 1843. He was united in marriage to Anna Louise Stone, Jan. 1, 1861. To this union were born two children, William Casper Butler and Juliet Butler Mayfield. His wife and both children predeceased him. He is survived by two grandsons, Theo Butler and Robert Mayfield, and two great-grandchildren, David Alexander Butler and Caroline Ann Mayfield, all of Stony Point, and a host of friends and neighbors.*
>
> *His Christian life endeared him to all who knew him. He had been a Lincoln County resident for his entire life and was the owner of the Butler Sawmill and a large section of timberland. He will be greatly missed by everyone he knew and everyone who conducted business with him.*
>
> *Funeral services were conducted Sunday at the Butler home at 12 o'clock and at the Stony Point Community Church at 1 o'clock by the Rev. Geo. Nevin. Interment was made in the Stony Point Cemetery.*

The picture of Paul Butler told Annie and Alice very little. It was blurry and rather small.

"That must have been taken well before his death," Annie said.

Alice grinned. "He looks forty-six, not seventy-six."

"Just what sort of man were you, Mr. Paul Butler?" Annie asked, looking at the man with fair hair parted down the middle and a solemn, earnest expression on his face. "And what did Theo do to make you take him out of your will?"

Alice looked thoughtful. "I suppose Jenny Thornton must have been related to Bonnie Mayfield. The article about the crash mentions Bonnie had a brother named Ralph. I don't remember Jenny's dad's name, but her grandfather could have been Ralph. He could have inherited the house from the Thorntons when they passed on."

Annie tapped her pen against her pursed lips. "The purse with the will hidden inside—it had to have been Bonnie Mayfield's. It had a comb with 'Bonnie' on it. Maybe her parents kept some of her things after the accident—her purse, a favorite dress and so on ... cherished reminders of a beloved lost daughter?"

"Yeah," Alice said. "That makes sense. And maybe, as time wore on, those things became the stuff that little girls played with."

Annie smiled. "Right. And with all the dress-up times between you and me and Jenny Thornton decades later, Bonnie's purse and other things must have been left at Gram's. But how did the will get into the purse lining? Why was it hidden?"

"If it was in favor of her husband," Alice said, "surely

Bonnie wouldn't have hidden it. But who else would have chosen Bonnie's purse for a hiding place? It seems unlikely that anyone would except Bonnie."

Annie frowned, thinking. "Maybe she hid it to keep someone else from destroying it. And who would benefit from the new will being destroyed except Ian's ancestor, Theo Butler?"

Alice whistled soundlessly. "This could be bad, Annie. You really should tell Ian."

Annie shook her head. "I'm not going to bother Ian with all my crazy speculations until I know more. He has enough on his mind as it is. Anyway, it's time for me to go pick up the twins."

"Annie—"

"Really, Alice. I have to get going."

She took Alice's arm and hurried her out to their cars. "I really appreciate you helping me with the research. And yes, I know. I have to tell Ian. Until I do, though, you have to keep this quiet."

Alice nodded reluctantly. "All right. I just hope you know what you're doing."

Annie gave her a quick hug and jumped into her car. "Me too. See you soon."

With a wave, she drove away. She *would* tell Ian. She would tell him as soon as she figured out exactly what had happened between the Thorntons, the Mayfields, and the Butlers in 1920.

~6~

They stayed busy all the rest of the week, and Annie didn't really have time to do more research on the will she had found. It wasn't until the next Monday that she had time to work on John's Narnian outfit. It was a challenge to get him to stop playing long enough to be fitted.

"Come on, John. Stand up on this chair and let me see how this looks."

John climbed up onto the kitchen chair, and Annie dropped the elf costume over his head and began pinning it to fit him.

"Grammy," he whined before very long. "When will this be done?"

Annie tugged at the bottom of the costume. "Stand up straight, John. I can't see if this fits right."

John pouted and squirmed. "I'm tired of standing here, Grammy."

"You've been here for two minutes. Really. Just be still a little while longer, and I'll be finished. OK?"

With a few more pins, she made the adjustments she needed. Then she pressed a smacking kiss to John's fore-head. "All right. You're done. And before long, you'll have a knight's tunic that would make High King Peter proud."

He grinned at her and jumped off the chair. "When will it be done?"

"I'll finish it as soon as I can, honey. If you don't have to have a lion on it, then it will be quicker."

"But, Grammy, it *has* to have a lion. I saw it in the movie, and it says so in the book."

She sighed. "All right. All right. I'll make sure it has a lion. A golden one—right?"

He nodded eagerly.

"OK." She pulled the tunic off over his head. "You run along and play with Joanna. I'll see what I can do about King Peter's tunic."

"Thanks, Grammy!" He reached up and flung his arms around her neck and then dashed out of the sewing room.

She had already removed the scarlet sleeves and the pointy green trim at the collar and around the hem of the elf costume. Now all she had to do was take it up and in to fit John and then add that pesky lion emblem. Well, she'd worry about the lion later. First she'd finish the tunic itself.

She moved a few of the pins and fastened some of the others a little more securely, then turned on her sewing machine. She had sewn about halfway down one side seam when the doorbell rang. With a little huff of impatience, she got up. Tunic in hand, she went to the door and opened it.

"Ian!" she said around the pins in her mouth. "I wasn't expecting you."

"I'm sorry," he said, leaning down and kissing her cheek, careful to avoid the pins. "I was driving past and thought I'd just drop in to say hi. Do you mind?"

"Of course not. Come on in."

"It's been kind of a tough day," Ian said, "and I thought seeing you would make it all better."

She beamed at him and stuck the pins back into the fabric just to get them out of the way. "You sure know how to make *my* day better."

"What do you have there?" He looked at the wad of red fabric in her hand. "Is this King Peter's infamous tunic?"

"Yes. So John's been telling you about it, huh?"

"No. Actually, it was Joanna." Ian shrugged slightly. "John doesn't seem to want to talk to me much these days."

Annie's eyebrows went up. "Still? Do you have any idea why?"

"Your guess is as good as mine. I tried asking him, but he wouldn't really tell me anything. I figured it was best to leave it alone until he wanted to talk about it."

She shook her head. "I'll see if he'll tell me. Sometimes he can be really moody."

"He hasn't complained about me to you, has he? I sure can't think of anything I did that might have upset him."

"No, not at all." She patted his arm. "Don't worry. It's probably nothing."

He nodded, smiling again. "So how is the royal raiment coming along?"

"It doesn't look like much yet." She held it up for him to see. "The tunic part is easy enough. I'm taking it up so it will fit John. But there's a lion emblem that's supposed to go on the front, and I don't have a clue how I'll do that."

"Hmmm." Ian knit his brows in thought. "Any idea what it's supposed to look like?"

"Not really, though John seems to have a very specific idea. He wants it to look like it did in the movie."

"Ah. May I borrow your computer for a minute?"

"Sure." Annie escorted Ian down the hall to the library, jiggled the mouse for her laptop, and stepped aside as the screen came to life. "Knock yourself out."

He sat down at the desk. She stood beside him, watching over his shoulder as he typed a few keywords into the search engine and pressed enter. Almost instantly, images of High King Peter's red tunic popped up, the golden lion emblazoned on its front.

"Will any of those do?" he asked.

"Hmm." She clicked on what looked to be the most likely one and then frowned. "I wish he was facing the camera straight on. And I wish the image was a bit bigger."

"Yeah. Let's see." He scanned the search results again and then clicked on one. "That's a site specifically for movie costumes. Maybe they'll have something."

He clicked around the costume site for a few minutes more and then smiled broadly. "How about that?"

"Oh, that's perfect!"

He had found a line drawing of just the lion emblem on a white background, and she quickly printed out a copy.

"I can use this for a pattern and appliqué the lion on the tunic. You're a genius."

She leaned down to kiss his cheek, giggling when he pulled her onto his lap.

"See? It's not so bad for me to drop by from time to time."

"Not bad." She slipped her arms around his neck and kissed his other cheek. "Not bad at all."

He was just bringing his lips to hers when they heard the pounding of little feet on the stairs. Annie and Ian both stood up.

"Mr. Ian!" Joanna bounced into the room, all smiles. "I didn't know you were coming to see us today."

"I didn't know I was either, cutie." He gave her a big hug. "Where's John?"

"Upstairs." She shrugged. "He said he was busy."

Ian glanced at Annie, and she could read the "I told you so" in his expression.

She gave him a warm smile and then leaned down to Joanna. "How would you like it if Mr. Ian stayed and had dinner with us, Joanna?"

"That would be nice. Are you going to have dinner with us, Mr. Ian?"

"Well, I hadn't thought about it." He glanced at Annie. "I didn't stop by to mooch a meal, you know."

Annie laughed. "I know you didn't. But since you're here, we'd love to have you. Unless you have other plans."

Ian shook his head. "I was just going to go home and stick some leftovers in the microwave and then watch a movie or something."

"Oh, you poor bachelor, you!" Annie slipped her arm through his. "You're more than welcome to have chicken and veggies with us. And we're going to watch movies over here too, if you'd like to stay."

Ian grinned. "If you're sure you don't mind."

"Hmmm." Annie paused, pretending to think hard. "I don't know. Do we mind, Joanna?"

"No!" Joanna threw her arms around Ian's waist. "Please stay and have dinner with us, Mr. Ian. We're going to watch a good movie later on."

"Oh, yeah? Which one?"

"*The Incredibles*. We watched it before, but it was really good, and John wants to watch it again. Parts of it are kinda scary, but I liked it too."

Ian glanced at Annie, one eyebrow raised, and she laughed.

"I bet you'll like it, Ian. It's a 'guy' movie, and it's pretty funny and exciting too."

"All right. I'm sold." He turned back to Joanna. "And then what?"

"Then I get to pick," she said.

"Ah-ha." Ian nodded wisely. "So then we'll get to see what? A princess movie?"

"No!" She cackled wickedly. "A monster movie!"

"Oh, no!" He pretended to be horrified. "Which one?"

"*Monsters, Inc.*" She hugged him around the waist again. "But don't worry. The monsters in that one are afraid of people."

"Whew." Ian wiped pretend sweat from his brow. "I feel better now."

Joanna giggled and tugged at his hand. "Do you want to see the picture I made? It's a picture of Mama and Daddy."

"Sure," Ian said, starting to follow her, but Annie stopped her.

"How about you go pick up everything you were playing with, and tell John to do the same. Then you can show Mr. Ian your picture. OK?"

Joanna made a little bit of a face. "All right, Grammy." She stepped into the hallway and shouted at the top of her lungs, "John! Grammy says to pick up now!"

Annie winced. "Joanna, I meant for you to go and tell him that. Not for you to yell."

"Sorry, Grammy."

She scampered off, and Ian chuckled.

"Sounds like she's having a wonderful time here."

"I hope so," Annie said. "I'm sorry John's still being difficult."

Ian shrugged. "It's puzzling, that's for sure. Like all this other stuff going on at the mill."

Annie put her arms around him. "Just forget about all that for a while. Just come and hang out with us for the evening. And when the twins go to bed, I'll let *you* pick a movie. How's that?"

He pretended to be unsure. "I don't know. What do you have? I'm a big fan of the classics."

"Me too. Come on. We'll take a look."

*   *   *   *

Joanna had fallen asleep about halfway through *Monsters, Inc.* John had dozed off right before it was over. Ian had helped Annie put them both to bed, and then they settled in to watch a movie of their own. Now Annie was about half asleep against Ian's shoulder, thinking how nice it was to have him there, making the big house seem not quite so empty.

The phone rang, and she sat up, startled. "Who could that be this late?" She looked up at the clock on the mantel. "It's after eleven."

"Want me to get it?" Ian asked, sitting up a little bit straighter too.

"No, I'd better." She picked up the receiver in the middle of the third ring. "Hello?"

"Hello, Annie? This is Reed Edwards. Sorry to bother you this late, but I'm trying to hunt down Ian. He doesn't answer his home phone or his cell."

"He's here." Annie glanced at Ian who was standing now. "We were just finishing up some buttered popcorn and *Casablanca*. Is everything all right?"

"I'm afraid there's been a little more trouble at the sawmill. Better let me talk to him."

She passed Ian the phone. "Chief Edwards."

"Reed. What's going on?"

Ian's brow furrowed as he listened. Every once in a while he nodded, adding an occasional "OK" or asking "Where?" or "How many?" Finally he sighed.

"All right. I'll be right out there. Wait for me." He hung up the phone and gave Annie a look that seemed equally apologetic and frustrated. "Sorry, Annie. I have to go out to the mill."

"More vandalism?"

"Somebody busted out all the windows on the east side of the building, the side opposite the one that faces the road. Anyway, I'd better get out there and see how bad it is. Tim was keeping watch and called the sheriff since it's his jurisdiction, and they called Reed because they couldn't get me at either of the numbers Tim had. Reed said he's going to meet me out there too. Sorry about the movie."

Annie gave him a sympathetic smile. "That's all right. I might have seen it a couple of times before. I'm sure John and Joanna are sound asleep. If I can get Alice to come over here while I'm gone, would it be all right if I come along with you?"

He managed a slight grin. "Another pair of eyes certainly wouldn't hurt anything. I guess with Reed and the deputy there, it's pretty unlikely whoever has been causing trouble will pop back up tonight. Go ahead and give her a call."

A couple of minutes later, Alice was at the door.

"Thanks for coming," Annie said as they walked into the living room. "I looked in on the twins, and they're sound asleep. I don't know how long we'll be."

"Not a problem. I was just working out my Divine Décor schedule for the coming month, and I brought that with me." Alice smiled at Ian. "It's just one thing after another for you lately, isn't it? I'm so sorry."

Ian nodded. "Thanks. Maybe we'll actually get a lead on this guy this time."

"I hope so." Alice glanced at the half-full bowl on the coffee table. "Oooh, popcorn. Mind if I have some?"

"Help yourself." Annie handed her the bowl and the remote control. "We'll be back as soon as we can."

Alice sank down onto the couch and tossed a handful of popcorn into her mouth, smiling at the paused image of Bogart and Bergman, their lips about to touch. "I think this is the beginning of a beautiful friendship."

7

"Ian! I saw them this time!" Tim Butler rushed up to the truck before Ian could bring it to a complete stop. "I saw two of them anyway."

Annie got out of the truck and then stood looking at the mill's office, its shattered windows sparkling under the red and blue lights of a couple of police cars and Ian's headlights. The bulb in the light over the back door was broken in the socket, and half a brick lay in the glass beneath it.

Ian came up beside Annie and took her arm, his expression taut. "Watch out for the glass, Annie."

"I saw them," Tim repeated, equal parts excitement and indignation in his face, and he pointed out into the trees. "They ran off through there."

"Ian." Reed Edwards came over to them, bringing a young officer with him. "This is Mike Harrison from county."

Ian shook the officer's hand and introduced himself. "Ian Butler."

"I understand you've been having trouble with vandalism out here for a while now," Officer Harrison said, looking at his clipboard. "Complaints filed on June 18 and 22."

"That's right. Nuisance-type damage so far. Like this." Ian looked from him to Chief Edwards and then back again. "Did they leave any clues this time?"

"We've got two different sets of footprints headed out into

the woods," Harrison said. "Can't tell much at this point, but it looks like we lose them in the creek back there. We ought to know a lot more once we have some light to work by."

"I was off in front," Tim said eagerly. "I heard the sound of glass shattering. I got back here as quick as I could, but they saw me and took off." His grin was suddenly a little unsteady. "You don't—you don't think they had guns or something, do you?"

"I don't want you to do anything dangerous, Tim." Ian looked at him sternly. "This isn't worth it."

Chief Edwards shook his head. "I don't think these people are trying to kill anybody, but you never can tell. Somebody could panic or throw something harder than he means to. You'd better just stay out of things, Tim."

"He's right," Harrison said. "If you see or hear anything, you call us. We'll take it from there. Got it?"

Tim ducked his head, somehow looking both disappointed and relieved. "OK."

"So what exactly did you see, Tim?" Ian asked.

Tim scratched the thinning hair at the crown of his head. "Well, like I said, I heard the glass breaking, and I ran around here. There were two I saw, but I guess there could have been more."

"We only saw two different sets of prints," Reed said. "And Tim's, of course." He led them a few steps toward the woods and shined his flashlight on the ground. "You can see one of them was bigger than the other."

"Those are mine over there," Tim said, holding up one foot a bit smaller than the boot marks left by the two intruders.

Annie bent down a little, studying the prints. All of them

seemed to have been made by tractor-soled boots of some kind. Not the same pattern, but the same sort of heavy workman's boot one would expect a construction worker to wear.

"I can see a lot of wear marks on Tim's. These others are both pretty clean prints," she said. "Like the boots were new."

Harrison nodded. "Seems like."

"Would vandals buy new shoes for the occasion and then dump them somewhere?" Ian asked. "Anything else, Tim? Did you recognize either of them?"

Tim shrugged. "I'm afraid I couldn't see much. They were wearing hats with the brims pulled down pretty low. Dark clothes. Nothing I could tell much of anything about. And I didn't get but a glimpse of them before they hit the trees."

"Short? Tall? Heavyset?"

"Yeah," Tim said. "One of them was kind of a big guy. Had to be over six foot tall and sort of heavy. Not really fat or anything, but a bigger guy. The other one was shorter and kind of thin. Like I told the chief here, I didn't much more than see them before they took off."

"Did they say anything?" Annie asked.

Tim turned a little red. "No, not a thing. All I said was 'Hey, you!' and I guess that wasn't all that helpful."

Ian sighed, surveying the damage. "All right, Tim. I guess you ought to go on home. I think the fun's over. For tonight anyway."

Tim shrugged again and looked down at the ground. "I'm really sorry, Ian. I thought maybe I'd catch one of them tonight or at least be able to see who it was."

"That's OK. I guess I'm going to have to hire some actual security until this all blows over."

"Aw, man, Ian. Don't do that. I can watch things here. I'll do better, I promise."

Ian gave him a pat on the shoulder. "I know you're doing your best, but I think we ought to put you back on the day shift for a while. Just until things calm down, OK?"

"Yeah, all right." Tim shrugged again. "I really thought I'd be able to find some clues or something. Especially since I actually saw them this time. Sorry, Ian."

Ian looked toward the ravaged building, jaw clenched, and Annie took his arm, hoping the tender gesture would help.

"What about inside?" she asked.

Ian turned to the two officers. "Has anyone been inside yet?"

Harrison shook his head. "Not yet. The door's still locked."

"I was going to let them in," Tim offered, "but they wanted to wait until you got here."

Ian gestured at the door. "Go ahead and open up."

Tim did so, and careful of the glass everywhere, they all went inside. Ian switched on the lights and looked around.

"I guess there's nothing to see in here besides broken window glass." He ran one hand through his hair. "There's no reason for any of this except harassment."

"Or maybe there's a message."

Annie motioned them all over to half of a brick that lay almost hidden under a chair. On it, someone had scrawled the letters "ICE."

Tim tilted his head a little to one side, forehead wrinkled. "Ice?"

"No," Annie said. "Look at this dash up here by the I.

It's too high up to be a hyphen, actually. It has to be part of another letter."

"Over here." Ian pointed to another brick half. "J - U - S and a T with part of the right side of the top line torn off. Not harassment. An agenda."

"Justice." Annie looked at him and then at Chief Edwards. "Justice for whom?"

"Don't touch anything," Harrison said. He began snapping pictures.

Once he had photographed everything, he donned gloves and turned the five other bricks over. One of them was broken like the first, but none of the other bricks had anything written on them.

"I guess that doesn't give you much to go on," Ian said.

Harrison frowned. "I'm afraid not. We'll dust the bricks for fingerprints, but I doubt if we find any. We'll also try to beef up patrols out here for a while, but you know how it is. We have a lot of ground to cover and not enough personnel."

"Yeah. Well, uh, thanks for coming out."

The two men shook hands again, and then Ian turned to Chief Edwards.

"You too, Reed. I appreciate your looking in on this even though it is outside city limits."

"No problem, Ian. Sorry I couldn't be much help."

Once the officers were gone, Ian gave Annie a half-hearted smile. "I guess I'd better get this all cleaned up. You want me to take you home first?"

"Don't be silly. Just tell me where you keep the broom. I'll sweep up, and you two can board up those windows until you can get Wally Carson out here to replace the glass.

Peggy told me a couple of months ago that his handyman work has been pretty slow, so I'm sure he'll be happy to have the business."

Ian's smile became much more genuine. "Thanks for helping, Annie. I knew there was a reason I fell in love with you." He gave her a quick hug, making her giggle. "Now, that broom is—"

"Right here." Smiling too, Tim handed her the broom and a dustpan. "And I think those plywood sheets we cut today would be about right to cover the windows—don't you think, Ian?"

Ian nodded. "You're a good man, Tim. Thanks."

Tim blushed faintly, ducking his head. "I just wish I could have stopped all this from happening. It's not right."

Ian gave him a pat on the back. "Come on. Let's get that plywood."

*   *   *   *

Annie yawned as Ian walked her up to the front door of Grey Gables. "Sorry about that. I guess it's pretty late."

"Yeah. Alice is probably asleep by now."

Annie smiled, linking her arm in his. "I owe her a big favor."

"So do I. She made it possible for you to come with me tonight." He kissed her. "I wasn't kidding before. It means a lot to me that you're always there when I need you."

"I didn't do much." She felt the color come up in her cheeks. "You've come to my rescue a lot more than I have come to yours."

He laughed softly, pulling her closer. "You don't have to *do* anything. It's just good to know you're there."

She slipped her arms around his neck, leaning up for a kiss, thinking it made all tonight's aggravation worthwhile, and then she pulled back with a little grin. "We'd better go in before Mom starts flicking the porch light on and off."

He chuckled and let her go. She quickly unlocked the door, and they went inside, making sure to be quiet.

"Hey, you two," Alice said softly, putting the DVD player on pause as she stood up. "I went ahead and started *Casablanca* over again since I hadn't seen it in a long time. Then I saw you had *The Maltese Falcon* too, so I've been watching that."

Annie hugged her. "Thanks so much for coming over on short notice like that."

"Not a problem. How are things at the mill?"

Ian shrugged. "Windows broken. That's about all."

"I'm sorry," Alice said, shaking her head. "This whole thing is crazy. Why would anybody do that?"

"We'll figure it out eventually," Annie assured her. "I hope the twins weren't any trouble."

Alice smiled. "Slept the whole time. Guess I'd better get to bed too."

The three of them went out to the front porch.

"I'll walk you over," Ian said, but Alice only shooed him off.

"It's just across the yard. I'll be fine. Nighty-night."

She hurried across the lawn and through the narrow copse that separated the two houses to her own porch; she paused and turned, giving them a wave, and then went inside.

Ian kissed Annie again. "I'd better go too. It's been a long night."

"All right." She hugged him tightly. "And don't worry. We'll figure it all out."

"I'm sure we will. After all, I have my own personal Miss Marple."

Annie laughed. "I'm not that old yet. Besides, you do your fair share of investigating too. Maybe we could be like Tommy and Tuppence instead."

"All right." He stole one last kiss and then pattered down the steps. "Good night, Tuppence."

"Good night, Tommy."

She stood there watching until his blue truck disappeared into the darkness. Then, with a yawn, she went inside, up the stairs and to bed.

* * * *

Annie sank into one of the comfortable chairs at A Stitch in Time. "Ahhh. It's nice to sit down for a minute."

Mary Beth chuckled. "You look beat. Are the little ones wearing you out?"

"It's not really that," Annie admitted as she fished in the bottom of her tote bag for her crochet hook. "There was more vandalism out at the sawmill last night, and I went out there with Ian to check it out and clean up a little. It ended up being a late night."

"That's awful." Gwen shook her head. "What was it this time?"

"Somebody broke out most of the windows on one side

of the office. Tim saw them this time, a couple of people in dark clothes. That was about all he could tell."

Alice looked up from the bookmark she was cross-stitching and grinned. "And I got to go over and watch *Casablanca* and the twins while they were gone."

"Where are the twins today?" Peggy asked.

Annie nodded toward the theater next door. "Ian took them to the morning show while we're having our Hook and Needle Club meeting. They're showing *Tangled*, and I think there's enough heroic adventure in that one to keep the boys happy."

Peggy grinned. "Oh, Emily has that DVD. It's cute. That reminds me, her birthday is Friday. We're having a party from two till four, and she'd like it very much if John and Joanna could come."

Annie smiled, not looking up from her crochet. "I'm sure they'd love to come, if you're sure you really want them. I know Emily is a little older than they are, and sometimes at that age, 'little kids' can be an annoyance."

Peggy laughed. "No, really. Emily always has fun with Joanna, and I wouldn't dream of inviting one without the other. As long as John doesn't mind coming to a *girl* party."

Annie lifted her eyebrows in mock horror. "Oh, we could never have that! He wouldn't be the only boy, would he?"

"Oh, no. Two of Emily's boy cousins are going to be there and several of the neighborhood boys, mostly with their sisters. I think there will be enough roughhousing to keep John happy."

"Well, I'll be happy to ask them if they want to come. I'm sure they'll be thrilled."

"Great. Unless I hear something different from you, I'll expect them Friday at two."

"Wonderful. That'll give me a couple of hours to run some errands of my own. They get bored sometimes with my 'Grammy stuff.'"

"Emily will be happy to have them," Peggy assured her. "Your 'humdrum' mystery must be heating up."

"It's pretty tangled," Annie admitted. "But I've never let that stop me before."

"Just stay out of trouble," Peggy warned her, chuckling.

Annie didn't smile back. "I'll try my best."

~ 8 ~

The following Friday, once she had dropped John and Joanna off at Peggy's house for Emily's birthday party, she returned to the courthouse to see if she could get copies of the wills of Robert and Bonnie Mayfield. Presumably they had left everything to their daughter, Caroline, but Annie thought it couldn't hurt to find out for sure. Maybe there would be something illuminating in how their property had been disposed of, some clue as to why Bonnie would have hidden a will that would have benefited her and her husband.

"Back again," Ms. Burke said when Annie came up to the counter. "What can I do for you today?"

"I need to get copies of two more wills, please."

The blonde nodded and handed Annie the forms she needed to fill out. "Excuse me just a minute while you're filling out those. I'll be right back."

Annie smiled and nodded, and wrote down the names Robert Paul Mayfield and Bonnie Marie Thornton Mayfield and their date of death, March 23, 1920. By the time she was finished and had counted out the appropriate fee, Ms. Burke had returned to the window.

"Thank you," she said as she took the money and the forms from Annie. "Now, if you'll give me just a minute, I'll have your copies for you."

Annie waited as the minute turned into five and then ten and then fifteen. Finally, Ms. Burke came back to the counter.

"I'm so sorry. We're having some problems with the printer, but I think I've just about got it fixed. Do you still want to wait or would you like to come back? I think it will be just a few minutes more."

Annie glanced at her watch. She still had time. The birthday party wouldn't be over until four.

"No." She managed a smile. "I'll wait. Thank you."

It was about twenty minutes later when Ms. Burke finally came out with her copies, apologizing profusely. Annie thanked her and then looked at the two wills. Neither of them was very helpful. Robert and Bonnie both had left everything to each other and, after that, to their young daughter, with Bonnie's parents as guardians and trustees. There was nothing there to tell Annie why Bonnie would have hidden Paul Butler's last will.

Perhaps she had been hiding it from someone who didn't want it to be made public. Perhaps that someone had thought it was worth arranging an "accident" to keep the will from ever coming to light. But who could that someone be? Who could it be besides Theo Butler, the one who had a considerable inheritance under the provisions of the old will? The one who eventually passed down that legacy to his heirs and, in time, to Ian?

She didn't know what the law said about such cases. Surely no one would even consider that Ian had done anything wrong, even if one of his ancestors might have. But would he suffer because of that wrong? Would his business be taken away from him and given to Cliff Bonds, the one who would own it now if this last will had been probated?

She had to tell Ian about this. She couldn't wait any longer.

She walked out of the building, and once she had put the copies of the wills into her purse next to both of Paul Butler's wills—the probated copy, and the one she had found in the attic—and the copies of the deeds she had gotten on her last trip to the courthouse, she started rummaging for her keys. They always seemed to settle under everything else in the bottom of her bag. When she didn't come across them right away, she gave the purse a sharp shake, and she got a reassuring jangle in response. The keys were down there somewhere.

"Come on now," she said half under her breath. "Come on, I know you're in there."

She gave her purse another shake and then looked into it. Ah. There they were. She reached for the ring of keys she saw peeping out from under her cellphone. Then suddenly her purse was stripped out of her hands. She grabbed at it, but it was already gone, and so was the ski-masked man who had stolen it.

"Hey!"

She charged after him, but he had already vanished around the side of the courthouse. When she got there, there was not the faintest sign of him or anyone. The street was empty. She checked the unmarked door in the side of the building, but it was firmly locked. The man had disappeared into thin air.

After she had taken a minute to catch her breath and

let her temper cool down, she went back into the courthouse and up to Ms. Burke's desk. No one was there, so she
tapped the little bell next to the nameplate. It was at least
two or three minutes later before the woman came back to
her station looking a little flustered.

"Sorry for making you wait. Is there something else I
can help you with?"

Annie nodded. "I've just had my purse stolen. Out in
the parking lot."

"Oh, no! Is there anything I can do? Would you like me
to call the police for you?"

"Yes, please, if you would. I'm afraid my phone was in
my purse along with everything else."

Ms. Burke called the police, but beyond taking Annie's
statement, there was little they could do. The officer admitted to her that in his twenty years on the force, he had found
that recovery of stolen purses and their contents was rare.

"May I use your phone?" Annie asked once the officer
was gone. "I guess I'm going to need a ride home."

"Sure." Ms. Burke turned the phone around so Annie
could use it. "You need to dial nine to get an outside line."

She dialed Ian's cellphone, not wanting to go through
his secretary, and Ian picked up on the third ring. "Hello?"

His voice sounded uncertain, and Annie wasn't surprised. He probably didn't get many calls from the Lincoln
County Courthouse.

"Ian, it's Annie."

"Well, hi there. I didn't think you'd be calling from
this number."

"I guess you can tell I'm at the courthouse in Wiscasset."

He chuckled. "Yep. What's up?"

"I was wondering if you could come and get me."

"What's wrong? Won't your car start?"

"Well, my car won't start because my keys are gone because my purse was stolen."

"What?"

"I just had my purse yanked right out of my hands by a guy in a ski mask." Annie smiled thinly at Ms. Burke, who was looking at her sympathetically. "If you would, Ian, I'd really appreciate it if you'd come and get me."

"Have you contacted the police?"

"They've already been here and taken my statement. I'll tell you all about it once you get here."

"Would it be better for me to stop by Grey Gables and get your spare set of keys?"

"Thanks, but to be honest, I'm so flustered right now that I'm not sure I'd be able to tell you where they are. I would rather come back for the car tomorrow."

"All right. Just tell me you're all right."

Annie's smile warmed. "I am. I'm perfectly fine. But I'd feel better if you were here."

"OK. I'm headed your way. Where will you be?"

"I guess I'll be here in the Probate Clerk's office." Annie sighed. "Hurry—OK?"

"I'll be there as soon as I can."

⁓ 9 ⁓

*I*an was as good as his word. Before long, Annie saw him striding down the hallway.

"Ian!"

Annie ran to him, and he wrapped her in his arms.

"Are you all right?"

Up until now, she had felt nothing but fierce indignation about the whole incident, but now she suddenly felt like bursting into tears. She managed a weak smile instead.

"Yes. But I'm glad you're here. Oh, Ian, I'm so mad I could spit nails."

He chuckled. "I have a feeling our purse snatcher is going to be sorry he ever messed with you. You didn't happen to recognize him, did you?"

"No. He was wearing a ski mask. As best I could tell, he was just … average. Not a big guy, not really tall, but not particularly little either."

"And you're sure it was a man?"

"Well …" She thought for a minute. "Reasonably sure. From what I saw, I think so. I did wonder for a second …"

He looked at her, eyes narrowing. "What?"

"Well, I was at the Probate Clerk's desk in the courthouse before leaving and having my purse snatched. Ms. Burke, the woman who had helped me, wasn't at the desk when I went back inside. I rang the bell, and she didn't

come in for a couple of minutes. When she did, she looked
a little flustered."

"You're not saying you think she's your purse snatcher,
are you?"

Annie shrugged. "I don't know. It seems pretty ridicu-
lous, doesn't it? I mean, maybe she's about the right size,
but I'm almost sure it was a man. And she's got this—"
Annie giggled. "Well, in Texas, we call it 'big hair.' It's teased
up pretty big, and I don't see how she could have had on a
ski mask just a minute or two before and it not be pretty
obvious. Besides, how crazy is that? A county employee who
pops out to steal purses on her break? She was probably in
the ladies' room or something."

"Yeah, probably."

Annie sighed. "I can't even drive my own car now. He
has my license and everything."

"It's all right. I'll drive you home. And we'll get you a
new license."

She pursed her lips, feeling angry again. "I'm going to
have to cancel all my credit cards and put a hold on my
bank account and cut off my cellphone and get new insurance cards and—Ugh! I can't believe this. I had only about
ten dollars in cash—maybe not even that much. I guess I
should be glad of that. But everything else—"

"We'll get it taken care of." Ian glanced at the Probate
Clerk's office door. "Are you all done here?"

"I think so. The police said they'd call if they find anything, but I don't think there's much hope of that."

Ian put his arm around her and walked her to his car.

"You didn't have your Social Security card in there,

did you?" he asked as he opened the passenger door for her.

She shook her head. "Thank goodness, no. But everything else. I—I just feel so foolish."

He gave her a comforting hug. "Why in the world would you feel like that? You didn't do anything wrong."

"Still, there should have been something—"

"You're the victim, all right?"

"All right." She leaned up and kissed his cheek and then got into the car. "All my keys were in there too. I can't even get back into my house. And I'll have to have all the locks changed as soon as I get home."

"Better get it taken care of right away. I don't want you and the kids to be by yourselves there until you do." He walked around to the other side of the car and got behind the wheel. "I hope Alice or somebody keeps a spare for you."

"Alice does."

They were quiet for a few minutes, and then Ian glanced at her.

"So what were you doing at the courthouse?"

"I was—" She gathered her breath and her courage. "I was doing some research on the probate of a will and some deed records."

"A will and some deed records?" He grinned at her. "Does this concern something else you found up in your attic?

She chuckled. "Actually, yes. Remember that day you were jogging on the beach and the twins were playing in the water and listening for mermaids?"

"Yes."

"Before that, we were up in the attic looking for some

dress-up clothes. We found a box with some things that looked like they were from the twenties—a dress and some shoes and other things. There was a purse in there too, a pretty beaded purse, and Joanna wanted to play with it. She accidentally tore the lining, and when I was trying to fix it for her, I saw that there were some papers hidden inside. Turns out, it was a will."

"Wow. Really?"

She nodded, watching his face as he watched the road. "It was the last will and testament of Paul Maxwell Butler."

"Butler? You mean, one of *our* Butlers?"

"Do you recognize the name?"

Ian shook his head. "Is he related to me?"

"As best I can tell, he was your great-grandfather's grandfather."

"Wow. That's pretty far back. Anything interesting in the will?"

She nodded. "Probably more interesting than you care to know."

His forehead wrinkled. "What do you mean?"

"I've been looking into this for a little while, Ian. Your great-grandfather was Theophilus Butler. You told me at the Butler reunion that he was the one who donated the land for Butler Park. In the will that was filed with the county and probated, Theo was the one who originally inherited the sawmill from Paul Butler, which was eventually passed down to you."

"That sounds about right. I can't remember all the names back that far. So?"

"Well, this will I found in the lining of the old purse was

dated two and a half years *after* the one that was actually probated. It was dated just two months before Paul Butler died."

He narrowed his eyes, obviously suspecting where this was going. "What does the one you found say?"

"It says—" She shook her head. "I'm sorry, Ian, but it says that Theo Butler was disinherited and he wasn't left anything from his grandfather's estate."

"What?" Ian's hands tightened on the steering wheel. "You mean—"

"Maybe you ought to pull over somewhere while I tell you about this."

He shook his head. "No, it's all right. Why—" His voice strained, and he didn't look over at her. "Why didn't you tell me about this will when you found it?"

"I'm so sorry. I—I probably should have."

"Probably?"

"Alice said I should have told you from the very beginning."

"You told Alice about this?" he said tightly. "You told her and didn't tell me? About something that could ruin my whole business? Something that could bankrupt me?"

She winced at the hurt in his voice. "I'm sorry. Really, I shouldn't have kept it from you. But I didn't want to worry you if it didn't mean anything. I didn't even know for sure Paul Butler was related to you until I did some research. And then I wanted to make sure Cliff Bonds got his timber property directly from the Mayfield side of the family. Please don't be angry."

He glanced at her, and then looked back out at the road. "I don't want to be angry with you, Annie, but how could you have not told me about this before now? It's just—this might mean the mill isn't really mine. Or at least it might mean it shouldn't ever have been mine."

"I know. That's why I wanted to be sure before—"

She broke off, hating the hard look on his face, praying that he could somehow forgive her.

"Sorry," he said finally, still looking straight ahead. "It's all a little hard to take in quite yet."

"I just didn't want to burden you with all this unless there was really a chance that it was genuine. When I left the courthouse, I was on my way to see you, to tell you about everything and show you what I found. I thought you ought to have the will I found authenticated. Now, of course, unless the police happen to find my purse, there's no chance of that."

"Hmmm."

He drove on for a few minutes, not saying anything. She decided he needed time to process what she had told him.

"So what happens if they don't find your purse now?" Again he glanced at her and then turned his eyes back to the road. "If that will is gone, what do we do about it? Is there any way to ever figure out if it's genuine or not?"

"I don't—"

"So we just pretend like it never existed and go our merry way?" His mouth was set in a hard line. "And be glad nobody can prove I don't really own the mill?"

"Please, Ian. It's a little early to start thinking it's completely lost at this point, isn't it? I mean, what's a purse snatcher going to want with an old will? What's he most likely to do?"

Ian glanced at her, eyes hard. "He'll take whatever cash you had. Your credit cards. Probably your driver's license. Your keys, of course."

"Yeah. It wouldn't be hard for someone to get my address from my ID and then come ransack Grey Gables."

He nodded. "Or drive off with your car. Once he has everything he can possibly use, he would probably toss the rest into a dumpster or something. It's not very likely it will be found at that point."

With a sigh, she leaned her cheek on her hand and stared out the window, not seeing the scenery that flew by.

"Where are John and Joanna?" he asked finally.

"Over at Peggy's for the afternoon. It's Emily's birthday, and they're having a big bash with cake and games and everything. I thought it was especially sweet of her to invite the twins since she's a little older than they are."

"She's a good kid," Ian said, his voice softening only slightly. "When are you supposed to pick up the twins?"

Annie glanced at her watch. "I'm late already. Do you think you could—"

"I'll be happy to take you over to get them."

Annie took a deep breath, especially thankful now for Emily's party. "I'm certainly glad they weren't with me at the courthouse."

Ian's expression turned especially fierce. "I already want to wring that joker's neck for what he did to you. If he would've scared those kids, I'd be hunting him down myself right now."

Annie bit her lip. Ian the protector, the knight in shining armor—he would have made a wonderful High King

Peter. She hoped she hadn't spoiled everything with him by keeping the will a secret.

"Sooooo ... what would work for you?" Annie asked. "Should we go ahead and pick up the kids? Or should I ask Peggy if she would let them stay a while until I get things sorted out?"

"I guess you'd better find out if you can get into your house first. You said Alice has a key, right? Is she at home?"

"Oh, I didn't think of that. If she's off at one of her parties, it might be a while before I can get in. Maybe I'll need a locksmith first thing."

Ian took his cellphone off his belt and handed it to her. "Why don't you give her a call, and we'll make plans from there?"

Annie punched in Alice's number; she didn't look at Ian as she listened to it ring.

Finally Alice picked up. "Hi, Alice, it's Annie."

"Annie? I was sure this was Ian calling."

"Well, I'm using his phone because I can't use mine."

"What's wrong?" Alice asked. "Didn't charge it up?"

"Well, my phone is in my purse. And my purse is gone."

By the time she had told Alice the whole story, they were pulling up to Grey Gables. Alice was waiting on the porch with Annie's spare key. She gave the key to Annie along with a big hug.

"I'm glad you're OK."

Annie gave her a lopsided smile. "I am too. I'm still a little shaken, but I think I'm more angry than anything. Right there at the courthouse and in broad daylight and everything!"

"Maybe the police will catch him," Alice ventured. "Do you want me to come in and stay with you for a while?"

Annie nodded, trying not to cry when Ian did not offer the same. "If you would. The kids are at Peggy's, and I need to see if she can keep them for a while longer."

"I'd better go," Ian said, not looking at Annie. "I'll call you."

"All right," Annie said softly. "Thanks for your help."

In another minute he was gone, and Alice was staring at her.

"What was that about?"

Annie blinked hard. "Let's go in, OK? You can help me figure out which credit cards I need to cancel and what else I need to do to try to save my money, my identity, and my sanity."

"Sure, but Ian—"

Annie pulled Alice inside and shut the door. She walked into the living room and dropped onto the couch and covered her face with her hands.

"Oh, Alice, you were right. I should have told him about the will as soon as I found it. I told him all about it when he came to pick me up at the courthouse. Now ...."

Alice cringed slightly. "Pretty mad, huh?"

"I hope he'll cool off soon, but yeah. I didn't mean to hurt him. I was trying to help."

Alice put one arm around Annie's shoulders. "He'll calm down. He's a pretty laid-back guy, and he's crazy about you. He knows your heart was in the right place."

Annie blotted her tears with the back of her hand and managed a smile. "I hope so. Now I'd better call Peggy and see about the twins. Then I can figure out what I'm going to do about everything that was in my purse."

Peggy was happy to let the twins stay at her house for as long as Annie needed them to. Soon, Annie had all her financial records spread out on the kitchen table. She had a stack of old bills and her latest bank statement.

"I guess there's nothing to do but start calling these places. I probably should start with the locksmith and then the bank."

Alice nodded. "If they use your debit card, they could clean you out in less than a minute."

With a sigh, she reached for the telephone. Just as she touched it, it rang.

"Hello?"

"Hello. I'm trying to reach a Mrs. Annie Dawson. Are you Mrs. Dawson?"

"Yes, I am. Who's calling please?"

"This is Sergeant Downs from the Wiscasset Police Department. I understand you were the victim of a purse snatcher today."

"Yes, I was." Annie looked over at Alice and mouthed the word "police" at her. "Is there something else I need to do?"

"No, Mrs. Dawson. Actually, I have some good news for you. I've never known this to happen as long as I've been on the force, but we've already found your purse."

Annie beamed at Alice. "Found it? Already? But how—"

"It was thrown into some bushes not even a block from the courthouse. Even more unusual than that, it looks as if your credit cards and ID and even your cash are still inside."

"You're kidding." Annie shook her head, her smile growing brighter. "Everything's there?"

"Of course, we don't know for certain yet, but there

is ten dollars and eighty-seven cents in cash, a bank card, three credit cards, your driver's license and your proof of car insurance. You'll have to check it out to see if anything specific is missing, but we find those are usually the things the typical purse snatcher takes. You can come and pick up your purse anytime at the station."

Annie thanked the officer and hung up. "It's amazing. It really is."

Alice grinned at her. "Do you think your thief had a twinge of conscience or something?"

"I don't know. Why go to all the trouble to steal a purse if you don't take anything out of it?"

"I don't know," Alice said, "but at least you'll be able to find out about the will too. It would be awful for Ian not to know for sure whether or not it was genuine." She glanced at her watch. "If you want to, we can go get your purse now, and then you can go over to Peggy's to get the twins."

"Thanks, Alice. Sorry to be so much trouble."

Alice took Annie's arm and hauled her to her feet. "No trouble at all. Now come on. We don't want to keep the twins waiting."

~ 10 ~

The trip back to Wiscasset was quick, and before long, they were at the police station. Annie signed all the appropriate forms and then waited for the officer at the desk to bring out her purse. She felt a huge rush of relief when she saw the familiar black leather bag. What a miracle it was that, unless the police were mistaken, everything was still safely inside.

The minute she had her hands on it, she started rummaging inside. Cellphone—yes; car and house keys—yes; wallet with ten dollars and change, driver's license, and bank card—yes, yes, and yes. And the will—

She looked up at Alice.

"The will isn't here." Annie dug through her purse again, just to make sure. "Alice, the will I found and the copies of the other documents aren't here." She turned to the young officer at the desk. "There wasn't anything else in here when it was found, was there? Some papers?"

The officer shook his head. "No, ma'am. We wouldn't have taken anything out or separated it from the rest. That's just how it was found."

Alice knit her brow. "Does your report say exactly where it was found?"

The officer checked. "All it says is 'in the bushes on the side of the courthouse, one hundred yards from the street.'"

Alice thanked him and took Annie's arm. "Come on. Maybe the papers fell out of the purse for some reason, and they're still there."

Annie frowned. "That doesn't seem very likely, does it?"

"We won't know if we don't look, will we?" She smiled faintly. "We're going to feel pretty silly if the papers are just lying there in the grass."

They weren't.

Annie and Alice looked in the bushes around the courthouse. Then they looked in the parking lot, around the trees, and even in the bushes growing next to the church next door. There was no sign of anything.

"I guess that settles it then." Annie sighed and leaned against Alice's car. "Whoever took my purse wasn't just an everyday purse snatcher. He was looking for that will specifically."

Alice thought for a moment. "OK, it should be pretty easy to narrow down the suspects then. Who knew you had the will?"

"Nobody." Annie shook her head. "Besides you, I didn't tell anyone. As I said, I didn't want to bother Ian with it until I had more to go on. I certainly didn't want anyone else to know before he did."

"You didn't tell anyone you were researching family records or anything?"

"No."

Alice frowned. "Somebody knew exactly what he was looking for, Annie. That's a little scary."

Annie nodded. "I'll be careful. I promise."

They took another quick look around the parking lot again and then went to Annie's car.

"I guess I'll catch up with you later then. You probably should still cancel your credit cards and all that, just to be safe, in case this guy got any of the numbers or anything."

"Good idea." Annie smiled at Alice as she got in her car and buckled her seatbelt. "Thanks for all your help."

"No problem," Alice assured her. "Let me know if you need anything."

Annie gave her a crooked smile. "If I can't get things worked out with Ian, I might need a shoulder to cry on."

"I have that too," Alice said. "Hang in there."

With a little wave, she hurried to her own car and drove away. Annie sat there behind the wheel for a moment, trying to slow her whirling thoughts. Then she started the car and headed down the highway. When she reached Stony Point, she drove directly to Peggy's house.

"Look, Grammy!" John ran up to her as soon as she came in the door, showing off the paper crown he was wearing. "I got it for being the best at hide-and-seek. If we play Narnia again, I can wear it when I'm High King Peter."

"Oh, wonderful," she gushed, giving him a congratulatory hug. "I guess you had a good time, huh?"

"Yeah, it was pretty fun." John made a face. "But Emily got a bunch of girl stuff."

"Because she's a girl, silly," Joanna reminded him, and then she flung herself into Annie's arms. "I almost won pin the tail on the donkey, but one of the bigger kids was better."

"Maybe next time you'll win," Annie said, hugging her tightly. "But I bet you had fun anyway."

Joanna grinned. "We had lots of fun. Em had the best

cake ever. It looked like a giraffe, and it was wearing a pink tutu and a sparkly tiara."

Annie laughed. "I wish I'd seen that! Now, I want you two to go find Emily and tell her thank you for inviting you to her party and for letting you stay to play after."

The twins scurried off, and Peggy came over to Annie, looking exhausted but happy. "I took pictures of the cake while it was still in one piece. I'll show them to you if I figure out what happened to my camera. I'm sure it's here under the disaster somewhere."

"Thanks so much for watching the twins for me while I took care of things with the police. Can I help you clean up?"

Peggy shook her head. "No, no. We can handle it." She frowned slightly. "But isn't that your—"

Annie glanced at the bag over her shoulder and then laughed. "Yes. It was the strangest thing, but the police found my purse thrown into the bushes. The only thing the thief took were some old records I was researching."

"Well, that's funny."

"A little scary, actually. That means it wasn't just a random thing, and the man knew what he was after."

"Do be careful when you're out, OK? Especially with the twins."

Annie glanced over to where John and Joanna were talking to the birthday girl. "I will. I don't want them to know anything happened, by the way. It'll only worry them, and it's all over now."

Peggy nodded. "Sure thing. And if you ever want me to

look after them when you need to do something, if I'm not working or anything, I'd be happy to. I think Joanna and Emily had an especially good time together."

Annie hugged her. "You're the best, Peggy. Thank you. Come on, kids. Time to go."

The twins bounced up to her, each taking one of her hands, and she hurried them out to the car.

"I don't suppose either of you is going to want any dinner tonight after all that cake."

"I do!" John grinned at her. "And I had two pieces of cake and some bubble gum."

"No wonder you're so rambunctious."

John's forehead wrinkled. "What's 'ranbunches'?"

Annie laughed. "That's *rambunctious*, and it means you'll probably still be wound up by midnight tonight. Now come on, let's go home."

*　　*　　*　　*

After they finished eating, John and Joanna went upstairs to play. Annie cleared the table and put the leftovers into the refrigerator. She was just finishing loading the dishwasher when the telephone rang. Her stomach churned when she saw the number on the caller ID.

She waited for another ring, trying to control her shaky breathing, and then she picked up. "Hello, Ian."

"Hi." He didn't say anything for a moment, and then he drew an audible breath. "I'm sorry I didn't handle things better this afternoon, Annie. It just—it took me by surprise."

"I know, and I'm so sorry I didn't tell you about the will

right away. I was just trying to find out all I could before worrying you about it."

"I know. I know." Again he was silent. "I'm sorry about your purse and things too, Annie. Did you get all your credit cards and bank accounts taken care of?"

She laughed softly. "It's the most amazing thing. I was in the middle of seeing to all that when the police called and said they had already found my purse."

"No!" He chuckled. "Cleaned out, I guess?"

"No, the only thing missing was the will I found and some copies of the other will and deeds I had made."

There was dead silence from the other end of the line. "Ian?"

"Then somebody knew exactly what you had." Ian's voice was grave and worried. "You really need to be careful, Annie."

"I will. Believe me." She paused a moment. "How much do you know about your family history? I mean, had you ever heard anyone mention Theo Butler or Robert Mayfield before now?"

"Theophilus, yeah. He was my dad's grandfather. But Mayfield? Not that I can remember. I've never really been much for genealogy. I can tell you the names of four of my eight great-grandparents—the ones on my dad's side of the family—but that's about it. I don't actually know much about them. Theo was born in Stony Point, of course. Why?"

"I was hoping you had heard some stories about family quarrels or things like that. That will I found said Theo wasn't included in the inheritance 'for reasons of which he is well aware.' Any idea what that could mean?"

"Hmmm." Ian paused, considering. "Nothing I can think of right now."

"You never heard of any scandals or anything in the family?"

He chuckled. "I think in the 1920s they were a lot more closemouthed about that sort of thing. You know who we might want to talk to is my Aunt Minnie."

Annie grinned. "I didn't know you had an Aunt Minnie. Who's she?"

"Well, to tell the truth, she's not really my aunt. She was married to my grandfather's brother, my Great-Uncle Danny, but he died when his plane crashed the day my dad was born. Grandpa was supposed to go up with him that day and didn't because Dad was expected to show up any time. Anyway, Aunt Minnie married somebody else a few years later, but she was always part of the family. If anybody knows anything about those days, she'd be the one."

"She must be pretty old by now. What year was your dad born?"

"1935," Ian said.

"So if she was old enough to marry in '35, she must be ... ?"

"Yeah. Umm ... ninety-something, I'm sure. But she's smart as a whip. I mean, as long as you don't ask her about anything too recent. If anybody still knows about Butler family squabbles back that long ago, it's Aunt Minnie."

"Do you think she might know something about Theo and Robert, and why Theo might have been left out of the will?"

"If you'd like, we can sure call her up. If she says it's OK, we'll go ask her."

"That'd be great." Annie caught a steadying breath, and then said, "Ian, are we—are we OK now? I'm so, *so* sorry about not telling you everything right away. I realize I should have."

"I know, Annie. And, yes, we're OK. But I really need to find out what's going on with the will and with whoever stole it from you."

"I'd love it if you helped me investigate," Annie said.

"I will. As soon as I can I'll talk to Aunt Minnie and see when we can pay her a visit. How's that?"

"Perfect. Thanks, Ian."

"Talk to you soon, Annie. Good night."

"Good night."

Annie hung up the phone and sank into a chair. Things with Ian weren't quite back to normal yet, but at least now it seemed that they would be. That put a smile on her face.

*   *   *   *

Annie was just putting away the Saturday morning breakfast dishes when the telephone rang. She smiled, suspecting that at this hour, it would likely be LeeAnn's daily call. A glance at her caller ID told her she was right.

"LeeAnn!"

"Morning, Mom. How are things there?"

"Oh, buzzing as usual. How about there?"

There was just the tiniest hesitation before LeeAnn answered. "Oh, we're just fine."

"LeeAnn?"

"Yes?"

"I'm your mother. I know when you are and aren't just fine."

LeeAnn laughed softly. "I guess you always have."

"So tell me what's not fine."

"Oh, it's this thing with Herb and his job." LeeAnn sighed. "We had a big discussion about it last night, and I'm really worried about what he's going to do."

"Discussion?" Annie asked. "Or fight?"

"No, it wasn't a fight," LeeAnn assured her. "We just talked. Or I should say *Herb* talked, and I listened."

"And what did he have to say?"

"Oh, Mom!" LeeAnn wailed.

"What, honey?"

"He wants to sell our house and move into this little shack of a place out in the middle of nowhere."

Annie gasped. "What?"

"One of his friends has a place he'll let us live in for free. Herb thinks if we live there for a couple of years, we can save up enough money for him to buy a business of his own."

"But how would he get to work every day?" Annie asked.

"It would be about an hour-and-a-half drive each way, but he says he could do it. The place is about ten miles from the nearest town, if you can call it a town. It's got a post office and a little bait shop with a sandwich place inside and a few groceries. That's it until you go another six or seven miles to get to a town that actually has a diner and a feed store and a real grocery. Not one of the major chains, mind you, just a little mom-and-pop place that hasn't been updated since about 1925."

LeeAnn had grown up in the suburbs. She had never

lived anywhere else. Annie couldn't imagine her out in the country. And in a shack?

"What about the house, honey?"

LeeAnn laughed faintly. "It's at the end of a mile-long gravel road. It's just a little clapboard house, probably built about 1930. It does have indoor plumbing and electricity, but there's no heat or air conditioning. There's only one bathroom, and that's just barely big enough for a sink, a toilet, and a shower. The bedroom, and there's only one, is exactly the size of our bed. By that, I don't mean it's the perfect size to put our bed into; I mean the whole room is exactly as wide and as long as our bed. There's a tiny loft at the top of the house. That would have to be where the twins sleep. The kitchen is just a sink, a stove, and a refrigerator in one corner of the living room. It's—oh, Mom!"

Annie could hear the tears in her daughter's voice and wanted so much to be able to hug her tightly. "Oh, honey, I don't know what to tell you. Could you fix the place up at all?"

"Mom! What difference would it make if we fixed it up? What difference would it make if it were a forty-room mansion? I would still be out in the middle of nowhere with Herb an hour and a half away at best."

"I don't know how happy I'd be, thinking about you and the twins being out there alone most of the time."

"It scares me to death. But he promises me it won't be for a long time. Just a year or two. Just till we can get some money saved up."

Annie's heart sank at the idea of LeeAnn and the twins having to live under such conditions, even temporarily. "Have you told Herb how you feel about this?"

"Oh, yes. We've talked about it a lot. And he assures me he won't do it if I'm really set against it. But when I see how much he's been wanting to do something like this, to strike out on his own and all that, I hate to say no. Especially if it's just for a little while."

"Well, I can't tell you what to do, honey." Annie refrained from sighing. "You and Herb have to do what's best for you and the twins, whatever that is. And sometimes— no, *always*—we *always* have to sacrifice to get something we really want. Does Herb know what kind of business he'd like to start?"

"Not really." LeeAnn exhaled heavily. "I guess I shouldn't be upset about this right now. We haven't done anything. We haven't decided anything. He tells me all the time that he's just throwing out ideas—just things for us to think about."

"Well, there's certainly no harm in that. Talking about what you want to do, exploring ideas and possibilities, those are good things, aren't they?"

"Yes." There was a reluctant touch of a smile in LeeAnn's voice now. "And I'm glad he wants to make things better for us if he can. I just don't know if all the trouble is worth it. I'd rather he got a regular paycheck and be home nights and weekends."

"Try not to worry about something that hasn't happened yet, honey. And it's something that might never happen. As your Great-Grandma Betsy used to say, 'Don't trouble trouble till trouble troubles you.'"

"Right." LeeAnn laughed. "You know, I wasn't planning on telling you all this stuff this morning. I really just called up to talk to the twins."

"I thought you had. But you know I'm always willing to listen if you need to talk. And that's true anytime."

"Thanks, Mom."

Annie smiled even though she knew LeeAnn couldn't see her. "OK, let me go get—"

"Mommy!" Joanna squealed as she ran into the kitchen. "Is it Mommy? Can I talk to her?"

Annie handed Joanna the phone.

"Mommy! I went to Emily's birthday party yesterday. The cake looked like a giraffe in a ballerina dress!"

Annie went back to loading the breakfast dishes into the dishwasher and listened to Joanna's happy chatter. She was glad she had the twins with her while Herb and LeeAnn worked out what they were going to do. There was no use getting the kids all stirred up when nothing had been decided yet. She prayed that when they did reach some decision, it would be a wise one.

~ 11 ~

nnie showed up early the next Tuesday morning for the Hook and Needle Club meeting.

"Annie!" Mary Beth came around to her side of the counter and gave her a hug. "I didn't expect you for a little bit."

Annie smiled. "I hope you don't mind."

"Mind?" Mary Beth laughed. "Of course not. You know you're always welcome."

"Thanks. Ian took the twins to play mini-golf, and I'm supposed to meet them afterward for lunch."

"Ian's such a good guy. A real keeper."

"Don't I know it. He's been great about helping me out with John and Joanna when I need him to."

"Well, as long as you're here, how about helping me straighten up the chairs and get ready for the meeting?"

"Sure."

Annie and Mary Beth started pulling the overstuffed chairs into a more even circle, and then Mary Beth went into the back room to make some fresh coffee. Annie followed her.

"Mind if I ask you something, Mary Beth?"

Mary Beth grinned. "As long as it's not my hip size, fire away."

Annie chuckled. "Nothing like that. I was just

wondering what it was like here at the shop when you first opened. Did it take a long time to get the business going?"

"Actually, I probably had a better start than most small-business owners. Why do you ask?"

Annie sighed. "My son-in-law is thinking about starting a business of his own."

"Oh, that's exciting."

"Well, yes and no. He's interested in it, but I think LeeAnn is scared to death they'll just lose a lot of money and end up without a business anyway."

"That's always a risk. A lot of people just jump into something like that without really knowing much about how to run a business, or how long it takes to really get it going."

"How did you do it?"

Mary Beth poured a cup of aromatic coffee and handed it to Annie before pouring one for herself.

"My mother gave me the choice of working in the fashion business with her and my sister or striking out on my own. I used the trust fund she left me to get started." She smiled wistfully. "You know me, Annie. The high-fashion social scene was never my style. I wanted to live someplace quiet and friendly—someplace where I could relax and be myself and not just one of the Bennington-Brock girls. Melanie was made to be one of the jet set, but not me."

Annie gave her a warm smile. "So you took the money and ran."

"You know it. Of course, that was before Melanie started running things and the business really boomed, so the money I got back then wasn't all that much. But it got me my little house and something to drive and enough inventory and operating cash to get the shop going."

"I'm glad you had an easy time of it," Annie said.

Mary Beth laughed. "I didn't say it was easy. The first few months were a nightmare. I really didn't know enough about the business to even know what I didn't know! I didn't know how much of what kind of stock to order. I couldn't seem to find a sales assistant I could depend on. I didn't know how to organize things so I could keep track of them."

"But the shop is great! It's set up beautifully, so welcoming and so attractive."

Mary Beth winked at her and leaned against the counter by the coffeemaker. "Well, I've learned a thing or two since I opened up. But there certainly was a long period when I wondered if I could keep the place going. I had a feeling my mother was waiting to say 'I told you so,' and that's part of what made me so determined to be a success. And, thank God, I did finally learn what I needed to know, and people finally started shopping here regularly, and of course, I hired Kate. I don't know how I could have kept the shop going without her. And now her crochet patterns are a big seller too, of course. Still, I'm not surprised most small businesses don't make it. It takes a lot of hard work and, I know in my case, a few miracles to get one going."

"And to *keep* it going. Poor Ian. His business was already long established when he took it over, but he still has his ups and downs. And now someone evidently thinks it's entertaining to see how much of a nuisance he can be around the mill."

Mary Beth looked alarmed. "Just how bad is it?"

"Oh, mainly vandalism. Broken windows, graffiti—stuff like that. Just enough to keep Ian worried all the time. Hundreds of dollars in damage, nonetheless."

Mary Beth shook her head sympathetically. "Kate often tells me she's glad she can just come in and work, and go home at night and not have to worry about anything else. Of course, with her pattern business, she still has to worry about reports and taxes and all that. But poor Ian. At least I don't have to worry about a lot of employees and federal regulations and men working with heavy equipment and sharp blades."

Annie took another sip of her coffee. "I guess all this at the mill will eventually blow over. He has the police looking into it, of course, but you know how it is. They're busy with more serious cases and don't have a lot of time for this sort of thing."

"*You'll* have to track down the perpetrator then, won't you?" Mary Beth's brown eyes twinkled. "He doesn't stand a chance."

Annie laughed. Just then, the bell over the front door jingled.

"Mary Beth?" said a familiar voice.

Mary Beth grinned. "That's Gwen. We'd better get out there."

*   *   *   *

During the club meeting, Peggy said that Emily was eager to have John and Joanna visit again, so they made plans for the twins to go to Peggy's later after she finished at The

Cup & Saucer. Annie called Ian to let him know she had a free evening, and they decided it would be a perfect time to go see his Aunt Minnie. Aunt Minnie was delighted to have visitors and invited them to come anytime.

Damariscotta Point Assisted Living was an upscale facility in Damariscotta, right on the river. Annie looked around the well-appointed common room, feeling a little amazed.

"This is really beautiful."

Ian grinned. "Yeah, her second husband, Marvin, did pretty well in the insurance business back in the day. Since they never had any kids, he pretty much spoiled Aunt Minnie and made sure she would be taken care of once he was gone."

He led Annie up the wide stairway and through the hall and finally to an apartment with the number 219 on it. His knock was immediately answered.

"Come in."

The voice was almost too low to be feminine, but Annie smiled at its warmth and friendliness. Ian pushed the door open and went inside.

"Aunt Minnie?"

"Come in, Ian. How are you?"

Minnie McArthur was a little tornado of a woman. Her hair was dyed jet black, but her bushy brows were white, and her eyes were a bright china blue beneath them. Watching her as she sat rocking and knitting furiously, Annie wondered if she ever slowed down enough to sleep.

Once Ian had introduced her, Minnie took Annie's hand in a warm, firm grip and gave her a wide smile. "So you're Ian's young lady. Well, aren't you pretty?"

Annie found herself blushing. "Thank you, Mrs. McArthur."

"Now, now. None of that Mrs. McArthur nonsense. You call me Aunt Minnie. Everybody does."

"Thank you, Aunt Minnie."

"Now, Ian, you get this young lady a chair so we can talk."

Ian did as he was told as Annie glanced around the apartment. It wasn't large, just a bedroom/sitting room and a mini kitchen and a bathroom through a half-closed door, but it was cheerful and nicely decorated. It definitely did not have the stereotypically bland, clinical look of a nursing home.

"This is nice," Annie said. "Really lovely."

"I like it," Aunt Minnie replied. "It's plenty big enough for me, and not much to keep up. And there's cable TV."

Ian laughed. "What else could you want?"

Aunt Minnie started her rocking and knitting again. "You know, if I've told Ian once, I've told him a dozen times he ought to find himself a nice girl to settle down with. He's too good a catch to be spending the rest of his life alone."

Now it was Ian's turn to blush. "You see why I haven't introduced you to Aunt Minnie before now?"

The old woman laughed, a surprisingly clear and youthful sound, and squeezed Ian's hand. "Now I know you didn't bring your girl to see me just to get my blessing. What is it you want?"

Annie glanced at Ian and then turned to Aunt Minnie. "Ian tells me you know a lot about the Butler family from way back."

The old woman's eyes sparkled. "How far back?"

"Nineteen-twenty?"

Again Aunt Minnie laughed. "Nineteen-twenty? Well, I was three years old then, but if you want to know something about apple juice and animal crackers, I can probably tell you."

Annie chuckled. "Actually, I was hoping you could tell me if you had ever heard about any kind of falling out between Theo Butler, Ian's great-grandfather, and Theo's grandfather, Paul Butler."

"Theophilus Butler? My Danny's father?"

"Yes."

Aunt Minnie pursed her withered lips, thinking. "Of course, this was well before I met Danny or any of his family, but I heard that some of them didn't really approve of Danny's mother. That would be your great-grandmother, Effie, Ian. I don't know how they could possibly dislike her though. She was always so sweet to me, especially after Danny died. She never had a bad word to say about anybody that I ever heard told, and I never saw anyone be anything but nice to her, but of course that was after she and your great-grandfather, Theo, had been married some years. Maybe things cooled down after Paul Butler passed away. I was just a very little girl at that time, of course, and didn't know any of them back then."

Ian glanced at Annie and then turned again to Aunt Minnie. "I never heard any of this before. Do you know why they didn't approve of Effie?"

Aunt Minnie looked around as if she were afraid she would be overheard. "Well, what your grandmother told me is that Effie had been engaged to Theo's cousin, Robert Mayfield, for nearly a year. Her family gave her the biggest wedding in Stony Point history up to that time. I believe she had a dozen bridesmaids and a string quartet, and the church was just bursting with flowers. I'm sure all the best people were invited."

"What happened?" Annie asked.

"Evidently she ran out of the church before she could say her vows. It was a terrible scandal, and even more so when she up and married Robert's cousin, Theo. I mean, back then, it was shocking that she would marry him at all, but doing it so soon!"

Ian frowned. "They married not long after she ended her engagement to Robert?"

Aunt Minnie wrinkled her forehead, her knitting slowing momentarily and then picking up speed again. "You know, I can't quite remember now what your grandmother said about that—just that everyone thought it was indecently quick. But I know she said Theo and Robert's grandfather Paul was not happy about having his family involved in such a public display. He was very particular about the family name and keeping things honest and aboveboard."

Annie glanced at Ian. Could that be the reason Paul had disinherited Theo? *The reason of which he was well aware?*

Annie asked, "Did you ever hear about how Robert handled it? Losing his fiancée to his own cousin, that is."

Aunt Minnie shrugged, still rocking. "I guess he must have gotten over it. He did marry and have a child. Of course, he and his poor wife were killed in a car crash when they were quite young."

"Yes," Annie murmured. "I saw an article in the newspaper about that."

Annie paused for a moment, thinking about that

article. *They seemed to be quarreling about something, but the subject of the quarrel was unclear. ... Recent concerns Mr. Mayfield made public in this newspaper might have been the topic of discussion. Police have found no direct cause of the accident.*

"Aunt Minnie, did you ever hear anything about why their car may have crashed?"

"Oh, no, honey. That was years before I married my Danny. Ian's grandma said his parents never talked about the Mayfields. I think there was some squabbling between the two branches of the family about their grandfather, Paul. I do remember her saying what an outrage it was that Robert had the old man dug up after he was buried just to make sure there wasn't any hanky-panky about his death. From what I ever heard about the old man, he wouldn't have been happy about that at all." Aunt Minnie shook her head. "Not at all."

"The article I read said the Mayfields may have been arguing before the car crashed. Did you ever hear what that argument might have been about?"

"Not that I can remember." Aunt Minnie shook her head. "What I remember hearing is that those two—Robert and Bonnie—squabbled a lot. Bonnie's parents would come and take their little girl to spend the night with them when Robert and Bonnie had one of their spats. Evidently Robert had big ideas, and she thought most of them were just foolishness."

"What kind of ideas?" Ian asked.

"Oh, I don't know, honey. Big ideas. Get-rich-quick sorts of things. I don't believe I ever heard any specifics.

There was something about drilling for oil back in 1918—that came up dry—and something else about some new kind of motorcar that ended up being totally useless. Mostly I remember hearing about their death, and what a shock it was to everyone when they were killed so suddenly."

Annie nodded sympathetically. "Do you know what happened to the little girl, Caroline?"

"I believe her mother's parents took her to raise," Aunt Minnie said. "They had a nice big house right on the ocean in Stony Point, I believe."

"That's down the street from where I live now," Annie said, beaming. "I used to play with the little girl who lived over there. Isn't that a funny coincidence?"

"Well, well. It sure is." The old lady stopped her knitting, made a quick count of her stitches and then started back at her furious pace. "Was she related to that part of the family?"

Annie nodded. "She was. I don't think the people who live there now are, but she was a Thornton, and Thornton was Bonnie Mayfield's maiden name."

"I knew they lived in Stony Point, but I wasn't sure where. I've been down that way a few times," Aunt Minnie said. "Not in years and years, of course, but I always thought it was pretty."

"Still is," Annie assured her.

"Anyway, I don't know if I remember much more of anything about that part of the family. I knew Theo and Effie, of course, and Ian's grandfather, David, and his wife. But before that, all I can tell you is what I heard from them secondhand. Of course, one of the juiciest stories, something nobody in the family would ever mention, was about the girl who killed herself."

Annie's eyebrows went up. "How awful. What happened?"

"Well, that's something I never did quite hear all the details about. Her name was Marlene Bissette. I remember because I thought it was such a pretty name, all French-sounding and romantic and tragic, of course. When I was a lovesick teenager, I wrote some terrible poetry using that name. 'Marlene, Marlene, her love unseen and shunned by him who would demean …'" Aunt Minnie chuckled. "Anyway, if I remember right, they said there was a squabble about her way back when. I wasn't sure whether Theo and Robert fought over her, or if one of them thought she wasn't good enough to associate with, or whether one of them thought the other ought to do right by her when he got her into trouble. One thing everybody agreed on was that Grandfather Paul was raging mad over it."

"But how did you hear about it if the family would never talk about it?" Annie asked.

"Oh, that was when I was just a girl, still in school, fifteen or sixteen maybe. I hadn't even met any of the family at that time. Some of the girls were swapping stories. We were each supposed to tell the most scandalous story we'd ever heard. Cassie Foster had an older sister who told her things she probably shouldn't have. She was the one who told us about Marlene." Aunt Minnie shook her head. "Of course, no telling how much of any of it was true. None of the Butlers ever mentioned it, mind you."

"I guess the family would have rather kept that particular story quiet," Ian said, glancing at Annie. "I suppose there are always a few skeletons in the family closet."

"Oh, sure." Aunt Minnie grinned. "Back a hundred and fifty years ago, one of my ancestors shot his own son dead because the young man objected to him living with a woman who wasn't his wife. They hanged the old coot for it too."

"Goodness." Annie put her hand over her heart. "Now I'm thinking maybe I don't want to know too much about my own family history."

"Truth is stranger," Aunt Minnie assured her.

Ian shook his head. "How come you never told me any of this before, Aunt Minnie?"

"You never seemed very interested in family history." She winked at him. "At least not the juicy stuff."

Ian leaned forward in his chair. "Well, I'm interested now. At least in the Butler part of it. Did they find anything … unusual about Paul Butler's death?"

"Not that I ever heard of. Of course, with the Mayfields dying in that crash so soon after, maybe the interest in Paul's death died with them."

Annie shook her head. "I read a newspaper article about it. It said that the family and the coroner both looked into it and didn't find anything but heart failure had caused Paul Butler's death. That's what the family doctor had determined as well."

"Well, there you are." The old woman smiled. "Probably nothing to it. You know, all I can tell you is what I heard the family talk about years after the fact. And I'm afraid my old memory isn't what it used to be."

Ian squeezed her hand. "You're doing just fine, Aunt Minnie."

"Thank you for letting us come and talk to you, Aunt

Minnie," Annie said. "You've been very helpful. Is there anything else you remember? About Great-Grandpa Theo or the Mayfields or even Paul Butler?"

"Hmmm." The old lady again slowed her knitting, trying to remember. "Not that I can think of offhand. But I'll sure think about it, and if I come up with anything, I'll let you know. And you feel free to call me anytime you think I can help you."

They spent a while longer with Aunt Minnie, mostly deflecting her questions about Annie and Ian's relationship and where it was heading. After promising to visit again, Ian and Annie drove back to Stony Point to pick up the twins at Peggy's house.

"It makes me wonder how involved Theo might have been in taking Effie away from Robert," Ian said as they turned onto the highway. "If she and Robert just had a falling out and she took up with Theo later on, that shouldn't have upset the old man so much. But if Theo actually went after her and broke up the engagement, Grandfather Paul might have been really offended. He seemed to be especially protective of the family name."

"That might have been the case," Annie agreed, "but I've been trying to figure out some dates here. When Robert and his wife were killed in that crash in 1920, they already had a nine-year-old daughter. That means they probably would have been married by 1910."

Ian shrugged. "Seems reasonable."

"But if that were the case, and Theo and Effie were married a year after Effie left Robert at the altar, that must have been before Robert married someone else. So, Theo and Effie were married at least by 1910, maybe earlier."

"OK. What's wrong with that?"

"Don't you see? If Grandfather Paul were upset with Theo because of Effie, why would he have made a will in Theo's favor in 1917? The one that was probated divided Paul's property between Theo and Robert. Whatever happened to make Paul disinherit Theo must have happened after 1917."

Ian frowned. "Yeah. Unfortunately, that makes perfect sense. So now we're back at square one as far as a motive for the 1920 will."

"We'll just have to keep trying. I'll check the newspapers again. Maybe there's something else—something between 1917 and 1920—that will give us a clue. Of course, as much as I hate to say it, if Theo was trying to kill his grandfather and his grandfather found out, that would be a pretty good motive for the old man to change his will, wouldn't it?"

"You don't suppose that reason might have been that girl who committed suicide, do you?"

Annie considered for a moment. "I was kind of wondering that myself. I just wish your Aunt Minnie had known a little more about her besides her name. I suppose this Marlene might have been involved with Theo in 1920. That would be after he was married and had a child. If that were the case, I can see how Grandfather Paul might not approve." She reached over and squeezed the hand that clutched the steering wheel. "I liked your Aunt Minnie a lot."

"Isn't she great?" He grinned. "I remember visiting her when I was a little boy. She and her second husband lived out on a farm a couple of hours away from us. We'd drive out there sometimes to fish and ride horses and things. And it never failed that she always had the best chocolate cupcakes ready for us. I don't know how she did it. I don't remember that we always called ahead, but she was ready just the same."

"Was she always such a whirlwind?"

"She sure was. She raised chickens and fed the cows and baked her own bread and all the other farm stuff, and she still had time to make her own clothes and knit up a storm. I guess the knitting is pretty much all she does now, but you saw for yourself she's not one to let dust settle on her."

"I just wish the situation with Paul Butler and his grandsons wasn't so long ago," Annie said. "It's hard to find much information on that. I mean, yes, you can look at deeds and wills. But the personal things—the motives behind why people did what they did—that's a lot more difficult. Your Aunt Minnie was a big help though. Thanks for taking me to meet her."

"I'm glad we went. She loves visitors, and she obviously liked you. Sorry she couldn't be any more definite about some of the things we talked about. But most of what she knows about the situation with Robert and Theo is just what she heard my grandmother say, and that was just family gossip from when my grandmother was growing up. Not all that reliable."

Annie nodded as they pulled up in front of Peggy's house. "I think I'll take John and Joanna to the library tomorrow. I should be able to find out more about Robert and Theo and Effie. Wedding dates and that sort of thing would be a matter of public record. For now, I'll just go get the twins, and we'll be ready to go home."

～ 12 ～

The first thing the next morning, Annie and the twins had a quick breakfast and then drove to the Town Square. Holding Joanna by the hand on her right side and John on her left, Annie walked up to the front door of the Stony Point Public Library. She stopped before going inside.

"Now, you remember this is a library and not a playground, right?"

The twins both nodded.

"I want you to have fun, but you have to be quiet so people can concentrate on what they're reading."

"We will, Grammy," Joanna pledged. "But they have a part for kids, don't they? And books we can read?"

Annie smiled at her. "They sure do, honey. I need you both to be extra good for a little while and let me do some research, OK?"

"Research?" John asked, narrowing his eyes in puzzlement.

"Research is when you need to find out something, so you go look in books and other records like they have at the library."

"Do they have research of everything that ever happened?" he asked.

Annie chuckled. "Not everything, I'm sorry to say. Only a lot of the public things."

"What are public things?"

"Public things are things that happen that everybody knows about. Like if somebody dies or opens a business or has a baby or gets married—things that might be in the newspaper."

"Are you going to look at newspapers?" Joanna asked.

Annie nodded. "Very old newspapers. About a hundred years old."

"When you were a little girl?" Joanna asked, a mischievous glint in her eyes.

Annie laughed and shook her head as they went inside. She waved at Grace Emory and hurried the children over to the colorful kids' section of the library. She saw a sign announcing story time was from 10 to 11 a.m. on Wednesdays. That was perfect. She'd have time to do some research, and then they could enjoy the story. She giggled to see that the book scheduled for that morning was *Ramona the Pest*. She didn't think the twins had been introduced to Ramona yet.

"All right," she told them. "Get yourselves a couple of books each that you can read while I'm doing research. In a little while, we'll come back over here, and someone is going to read a story to you."

"What are they going to read?" John asked. "About dinosaurs?"

"No," Annie told him, "but you'll like this story. I remember it from when I was your age. Now, do you see that little room over there?" She pointed toward the room beyond an archway on the opposite side of the Great Room. "That's the Reference Room, where they keep all the research materials. We're going to go in there as soon as you both pick out your books. And if you behave yourselves and let me do what I need to, then we'll go have hamburgers over at The Cup & Saucer and see Miss Peggy. All right?"

"Yes, Grammy," the twins both promised.

"And you'll remember to be quiet, right?"

John nodded and Joanna put one finger over her lips.

"OK. Now let's find some good books."

A few minutes later, the three of them walked to the Reference Room. With Grace's permission, they borrowed a couple of comfy cushions from the kids' section, and the twins sprawled out on them under the windows. Joanna was lying on her back, quietly making one of her books "fly" around her. John was sitting cross-legged on his cushion, reading something about Alvin and the Chipmunks. Annie gave them an approving smile and made her way over to the bank of computers.

A search of Lincoln County marriage records told her that Theophilus Alexander Butler and Effie Bernice Preston had been married on June 5, 1909. Robert Paul Mayfield and Bonnie Marie Thornton married on February 12, 1910. After jotting down that information in the little notebook she carried in her purse, she congratulated John and Joanna on their good behavior and then went to the microfilm reader. It didn't take Annie long to find the wedding announcements in *The Chronicle* for both couples.

Then she looked back through the editions of the newspaper before June of 1909. Aunt Minnie had said there was something of an outrage at how soon Effie had married Theo after breaking her engagement with Robert. Maybe Annie would be able to find something about that too. The paper came out only on Wednesdays, so that made it a little easier for Annie to search.

She decided to start with the Wednesday immediately before the announcement of Effie's marriage to Theo. It would be great to see if there was an announcement of their engagement too, and if there was any information she could get for that. But there was nothing at all in the May editions of *The Chronicle*. Nothing in April or March, February or January. Nothing until September 1908, and then, just a dignified announcement of the engagement of Miss Preston to Mr. Butler, with the wedding to take place the coming June.

Annie searched the archives for the months preceding the announcement, back to the previous June. There was nothing in the section that held the engagement and marriage announcements, but something in the June 30 gossip column caught her attention.

> ### PRESTON-MAYFIELD WEDDING HALTED
> *This past Saturday, the wedding of Miss Effie Preston to the dashing Mr. Robert Mayfield came to an abrupt halt when, after the groom had repeated his vows, the bride fled down the aisle and into a waiting automobile, leaving the church overflowing with stunned guests and her father, financier Mansfield Preston, footing the bill for what would have been the grandest wedding in Stony Point history.*
>
> *Miss Preston's getaway car took her not to some secret rendezvous, but merely to her own home, from which she has repeatedly declined to give interviews. The family of the groom has expressed their hopes that, despite this instance of maidenly trepidation,*

the couple will eventually be united in matrimony.

The family of the bride-not-to-be has declined comment.

Annie shook her head. So much for Effie's "indecently quick" marriage to Theo. It had been nearly a full year. She wondered now how long Effie and Robert Mayfield had been engaged. Aunt Minnie said it had been over a year. Maybe Annie could find more information about that.

She glanced down at the floor. Joanna had dozed off on her cushion, her little stack of books clutched to her chest. John was still looking at his chipmunk book.

"Hi, Grammy," he said, grinning and keeping his voice very soft.

She gave him a wink and a little wave. "It'll be time for story hour in just a few minutes. All right?"

He nodded and whispered, "And can we still go to Miss Peggy's for lunch?"

"You bet, honey."

Annie turned back to the microfilm reader, scanning back through the marriage and engagement announcements. Finally, in early August of 1907, she found what she was looking for.

PRESTON-MAYFIELD ENGAGEMENT
ANNOUNCED

Mr. and Mrs. J. Mansfield Preston of 1664 Bayview Drive, Pleasant Point, announce the engagement of their daughter, Miss Effie Bernice, and Robert Paul Mayfield, grandson of Paul M.

Butler, well-known Stony Point businessman. The marriage will take place June 27th of next year at the Stony Point Community Church.

The young people first met at Miss Mamie Barlow's popular community Christmas party, when Mr. Mayfield came home for the holiday from the University of Maine in Augusta, from which he has since obtained his Bachelor of Arts Degree.

Miss Gladys Stebbins entertained with a linen shower for Miss Preston Saturday afternoon at her home, 1659 Bayview Drive, Pleasant Point. Bride's roses adorned the rooms and the gifts for the bride were hidden in a large floral bell suspended in the dining room. A floral guessing game entertained the guests, who, beside the guest of honor, were Mesdames J.M. Wentworth, W. Peck, Willa Neville, Reba Tunnlson, T.N. Stebbins, Misses Frances Borgmier, Lucille Emery, Lois Hasson, Ethel Bronsen, Irene Holder, Isadora Petrova, Alma Stebbins and Mabel Stebbins.

Below the announcement was a grainy photograph of the bride-to-be. Effie Preston looked solemnly into the camera, her delicate brows almost imperceptibly lifted, her dark eyes almost pleading, her soft, sweet mouth turned down only slightly. Perhaps she had wanted to be happy about her coming marriage and couldn't quite manage it. Or perhaps the day the photograph was taken had been a difficult one for her and there was nothing more to it than that. Maybe her corset was too tight. After over a hundred years, it was impossible to know for certain.

But how lovely she was. Her dark hair, thick and lush, was upswept in a Gibson-girl style, her oval face and slender figure perfection, and she wore her fashionable clothes with grace and elegance. No wonder both cousins had been smitten by her. Annie studied Effie's image intently.

So, Miss Effie, what made you run away at the altar and marry Theo Butler later?

If only old photographs could talk.

There was a low, bell-like tone, and then a voice announced the beginning of story time in the children's section of the library. John looked up from his book, and Annie smiled at him.

"Let me just put everything here back the way it was, and then we'll go listen to the story."

He nodded and stood up. "I was getting pretty tired of being good."

"You did great," Annie said, laughing softly as she put the rolls of microfilm back where she had gotten them. "I'm proud of both of you."

Joanna sat up, blinking. "Did I miss the story, Grammy?"

"No, honey, it's just about to start. Get your books and your cushion, and let's go see what that pesky Ramona is up to today."

~ 13 ~

*I*an sat in his office at the sawmill, tapping his fingers on the top of the desk and listening as one of his most valuable customers tore him up one side and down the other because an order had not been delivered when promised.

"Yes, Mr. Rodale. I realize you placed your order two weeks ago. I apologize for the delay, but as Mr. Austin already explained to you, we've had a delay from our supplier. I promise you I will personally find out what's happening and get back to you with a firm delivery date."

Rodale only snorted. "That won't be necessary, Mr. Butler. This isn't the first time we've had a problem like this lately, and I don't have any more time to waste on your delays. You can just cancel that order. We'll find another supplier."

There was a controlled but definitely final click from the other end of the line. With a sigh, Ian hung up the telephone and went out to Max Austin's desk.

"What's going on with that timber for the Rodale order? It was supposed to be here four days ago."

Max looked apologetic. "I've called Cliff Bonds six times about that so far. All I can get out of him are vague excuses. Now he won't even take my calls. Should we try to get another timber supplier?"

Ian frowned. "Something must be going on over there.

Last time I talked to him, I could hardly get a word out of him. Maybe I ought to go pay him a visit."

"Good luck with that," Max said. "The past few days, Mayfield Timber has been making things miserable for us. Orders late. Orders lost. Orders wrong. Equipment breakdowns. Truck breakdowns. One excuse after another—or no excuse at all. Nobody over there seems to know what's going on. Or at least they all seem pretty dead set on not saying. I've worked with Connor Lewis for the past twelve years, and now he won't even talk to me."

Ian clenched his jaw. "OK, I'm going up there. I'll talk to Bonds or I'll talk to Lewis or I'll talk to both of them. We have contracts. If they don't want our business, they can at least tell us that."

*   *   *   *

Ian spent the drive up to the offices of Mayfield Timber Supply trying to get a grip on his emotions. It wouldn't help matters with Bonds or anyone else if he flew off the handle the minute he saw the man. Calm and steady was the only way to handle this sort of thing. Whatever the problem was, they could work it out in a way that was fair to both parties.

Ian slapped his steering wheel with a low growl. *This is crazy. All of it. And why does it have to happen just now?* Didn't he have enough to worry about with the vandalism and the break-ins and the equipment breakdowns and Annie getting her purse snatched and the questions raised by that will and everything else?

It still bothered him. Not the purse snatching so much,

though that was bad enough, but the idea that someone had deliberately stolen the 1920 will along with Annie's copy of the 1917 one, and her copies of the deed records and the other wills, and then left everything else. Those records were all related to Bonds's family as well as Ian's. Surely Cliff hadn't had anything to do with Annie getting her purse stolen.

Justice. Ian thought of the broken brick that they picked up off the office floor in the middle of all that broken glass. Justice? Did Cliff somehow know about the later will? If so, how? And what was he prepared to do about it?

Ian pulled up in front of the offices of Mayfield Timber Supply and was happy to see the black crew-cab truck with the license plate that said "BONDS7." Bonds was here. Ian would get to the bottom of these supply problems.

He found a place to park and went up to the front desk. The young woman there, who didn't look like she had been out of school very long, gave him a bright smile.

"Hello. May I help you?"

"I'd like to speak to Mr. Bonds, if I may."

She picked up the telephone on her desk and touched a button. "May I give him your name, please?"

"Yes. Ian Butler. He knows me."

She nodded and then put the receiver to her ear. "Monica?" she said after a brief pause. "There's an Ian Butler here to see—oh. OK. Well, I'll tell him. Thanks."

She hung up the phone and smiled again at Ian.

"I'm sorry, Mr. Butler, but Mr. Bonds is out."

So that was the way it was. Two could play at that game.

"What a shame," Ian said, and he managed to look

genuinely grieved. "I really do need to speak to him. Do you know when he'll be back?"

"I'm sorry, Mr. Butler, but, no, I don't. I'll be happy to leave him a message for you if you like."

Ian thought of a few extremely to-the-point messages he'd like to leave, but perhaps none of those would be very charitable. They certainly wouldn't be professional. He smiled.

"Yes, if you would. Just tell him Ian Butler came by to discuss the fulfillment of certain timber contracts for his mill." He rattled off his phone number. "And tell him I'll see him very soon."

She wrote out the message on her pad and then tore off the page and impaled it on the message spike on the corner of her desk. "I'll make sure he gets it, Mr. Butler."

Ian wished her a good afternoon and went out to his car.

"Two can certainly play your game, Bonds," he muttered under his breath as he pulled the car around to the side of the building where he could still see Bonds's truck but his own car was less likely to be noticed. "And I can be pretty patient when I need to be."

It was ten minutes till five. There was no guarantee, but he was hoping that the office closed at five and that Bonds would be leaving on time today. He waited, turning over in his mind what he would say if and when Bonds showed up, and finally, two or three minutes past the hour, people started coming out of the building, getting into their cars, and driving away. At about eight minutes past, he saw his cousin several times removed.

Clifton Bonds was perfect for the timber business. He looked just like a lumberjack, tall and burly and bearded, and, as Ian remembered, he had a rather colorful vocabulary. *This,* Ian reminded himself hopefully, *doesn't have to get ugly.*

While Bonds was still walking toward his truck, Ian slipped out of his car and hurried over to him.

"Hey, Cliff. Got a minute?"

Bonds turned around, startled, and then frowned. "Actually, I don't. I'm late already."

"I've been trying to get in touch with you or *somebody* over here for several days now. About the order we placed to be delivered on the twenty-fifth. Actually it's about a lot of things before that, but we can start there."

"We're closed right now," Bonds said as he unlocked his truck. "Besides, you need to talk to our orders department. Connor Lewis will be able to help you. First thing tomorrow."

Ian crossed his arms over his chest. "Well, that's exactly my problem. My manager has tried to call your Mr. Lewis about twenty times in the past three days. I've tried to call you at least that many times. Really, Cliff, what's going on? You're avoiding me. Admit it."

Bonds laughed humorlessly. "I don't know what you're talking about. Just because I've been really busy—"

"Why did you tell your receptionist to lie to me?"

"I don't know what you're talking about." Bonds scowled. "What do you mean?"

"I checked out your parking lot when I went in. Your truck was right here." Ian patted the black metal. "And when I came out."

"I never told her I wasn't in."

"No," Ian agreed. "You had your secretary tell her. Name's Monica, right?"

Bonds shrugged. "Must have been some misunder-standing once the message got to you. Monica told her I was unavailable, not out of the office."

Ian looked at him dubiously. "OK, we'll chalk that one up to a misunderstanding. Maybe now that we're actually talking, we can resolve all the other problems."

"No, not right now. I told you, I'm running late for something."

"Come on, Cliff. I just want to know what's wrong. Your company and mine have been doing business together for close to a hundred years. We've both fulfilled our ends of the contracts and, I'm pretty sure, made a decent profit from the relationship. Now, all of a sudden, what? Orders are missing? Deliveries are late or just not there? Nobody knows what's going on? Nobody can even answer a phone call? What's all that about?"

"I don't keep up with day-to-day stuff. You'll have to ask Connor Lewis—"

"You don't keep up with day-to-day stuff?" Ian shook his head in disbelief. "You're the owner of the place, Cliff. If you know there's a problem, then you get to the bottom of it. At least that's the way it works at my mill. If one of my people can't do his job, then it's up to me to put things right. You're not new at this. Why are you suddenly letting everything fall apart? I can't be the only one who has complained."

Bonds turned at last to face him, burly arms crossed over his chest. "Matter of fact, you are."

Ian stared at him for a moment, trying to read the sneer in his expression. "Are you telling me it doesn't bother anyone else for your company to ignore their calls and botch their orders and pretty much not care about keeping their business?"

"Nobody else has those complaints."

"OK." Ian nodded grimly. "I get it now. This is something just between you and me—right?"

Bonds just stood there, arms still crossed.

"Care to tell me what it is?" Ian asked finally.

Bonds's mouth turned up at one side. "You'll find out soon enough."

He pulled open the driver's side door of his truck, and Ian held his arm there.

"What are you talking about?"

Bonds glanced down at Ian's hand and then back into his eyes. "You don't really want to add assault charges to the trouble you're about to be in, do you?"

Jaw clenched, Ian released him and took a step back. All he could do was watch Bonds get into his truck and drive away.

As soon as he was gone, Ian went back to his car and punched Annie's number into his cellphone. She answered on the second ring.

"Hi, Ian. What's up?"

"That's exactly what I'd like to know. Mind if I stop by to talk for a little while?"

She hesitated for a second. "Sure, that's not a problem. Is everything all right?"

"I'm not sure." He turned the key in the ignition. "I'll see you in a few minutes."

~ 14 ~

Annie looked up from her meat loaf recipe when the doorbell rang. "How about if you two go let Mr. Ian in?" John, in the High King Peter tunic Annie had finally finished for him, made a face and kept on coloring his dragon picture, but Joanna grinned, jumping up from the table and darting toward the front of the house.

"I will, Grammy!"

"Ask him if he will please come into the kitchen," Annie called after her.

She stood listening as Joanna opened the door and said hello to Ian and very politely invited him in. She smiled to see Joanna lead him by the hand into the kitchen.

"Hi, Annie." Ian leaned over to kiss her cheek, and then smiled at her grandson. "Hello, John."

"Hello." John didn't look up. He was coloring what looked like a stormy sea below his dragon. "Grammy, may I be excused?"

Annie frowned. "John, you know Mr. Ian just got here and—"

"Actually," Ian said, "I really would like to talk to you alone for a few minutes. I think it would be best."

"Awww," Joanna moaned, tugging at Ian's hand, and he dropped to one knee beside her.

"It won't take long, sweetie, I promise. And then you

can show me your picture and tell me all about what you and John did today. How's that?"

Her expression brightened. "And will you come see our dragon?"

"Eustace? Sure. Wouldn't miss it."

Annie smiled. "All right, you and John excuse us for a few minutes. I have to finish the meat loaf while Mr. Ian and I have a little talk, but I'll call you when we're through."

John hurried out of the kitchen and Joanna scampered after him.

"Stay inside," Annie called, and then she turned to Ian, her expression turning serious. "So what's going on? You sounded grim on the phone."

"I finally got to talk to Cliff Bonds."

"Oh, really?" She pulled out a chair for him. "Have a seat and tell me about it. You don't mind if I keep making dinner?"

"Not at all." He sat down. "Sorry to interrupt."

She studied his face for a second. He looked a little angry, but mostly he looked worried and puzzled. She closed her cookbook and sat down next to him.

"Tell me what happened with Cliff."

He gave a startled little laugh. "What about your meat loaf?"

"It can wait." She put her arm through his and gave him a snuggling little squeeze. "It won't hurt anything if dinner is a few minutes later than I planned. Want to stay and eat with us?"

He shrugged. "I don't know. I think I might still be on John's blacklist, and with what's going on at the mill and all, I'm getting enough rejection right now as it is."

"I'm so sorry, Ian." She gave him another squeeze and then looked through the door leading out of the kitchen, the one John had just gone through, and shook her head. "John's going through some kind of funny phase right now, I think."

He chuckled. "Well, that's good. Can't have too many of us trying to watch out for you, you know. Not with all the trouble you get yourself into."

She shook her head, laughing. "I do not."

"Well, maybe not *too* much trouble. But that is sort of what I came to talk to you about. As I said, I actually got to talk to Cliff Bonds today. I went out to his office, but I was put off by his secretary. So I staked out the parking lot until he came out. He wasn't too happy about that."

"It's not as though you didn't try to call him on the phone a million times."

"There is that. Anyway, he wouldn't tell me anything but that I needed to talk to his manager about the orders we haven't gotten. He says he doesn't know about the day-to-day details of the business." Ian frowned. "I'm not buying that one. He's kept that place running well for more than twenty years. That doesn't happen by accident."

Annie nodded. "But he didn't have any explanation for you? About what's been going on?"

"No, but that's not what's really bothering me. I made the mistake of trying to keep him from getting into his truck, and he told me that with all the trouble I'm about to be in, I didn't want to face assault charges too."

Annie scowled. "All the trouble you're *about* to be in?"

"Yeah. And he took off before I could get anything else out of him. Now I'm wondering—"

"The wills," she said. "If that later will is genuine, then his family should have gotten the sawmill too. That has to be what he meant."

"I don't know what else it could be," Ian admitted. "That would explain his sudden hostility toward me and the mill."

Annie stood up and went back to her recipe, silent for a moment as she started putting ingredients into the mixing bowl. "So ... what will you do if we get the will back and it turns out to be genuine? If the Mayfields really should have inherited the mill too?"

Ian sighed. "I've been thinking about that for a while now. I don't guess there's much I can do. If it's his, it's his, isn't it?"

"You could get a lawyer and find out what the law says." Annie measured out the spices the recipe called for and added them to the ground beef and chopped bell peppers, onions, and mushrooms in the bowl. "I mean, it's getting close to a hundred years ago since your branch of the family got the mill. After all that time, don't you think—"

"I think it's only fair that he should have what should have been his or at least some kind of compensation for it. I don't know what a court would say is fair compensation, but it ought to be something." He propped his chin on one hand, looking pretty glum. "And I'd guess that 'something' would be pretty substantial."

"But your family has built that business up for almost a century. It can't be fair for you to lose everything like this. It's not your fault if the wrong will was probated."

He gave her a wan smile. "I think they call it 'unjust

enrichment.' Maybe I didn't do anything wrong myself, but I'm benefiting from something that should belong to someone else."

"*If* that will is genuine. We don't know anything of the kind yet."

He laughed softly, but there was no humor in it. "That's just it. We don't know. If the will is really gone, if whoever stole it from you has destroyed it or lost it or something, we won't ever know. I'm not sure I can just pretend all of this never happened. I'd always wonder if I had something that didn't really belong to me."

"What would you do?" She stopped her stirring, and her voice was very quiet.

"I guess the fair thing would be to figure out how much the mill was worth back in 1920 and pay him that. Adjusted for inflation, I suppose." He shrugged. "I don't have a clue how much that would be."

"I guess that adjusted for inflation part would be the real kicker after nearly a hundred years."

He didn't say anything for several minutes. "I don't know where I'll get the money." He looked down at the table, obviously not seeing it. "But there's really nothing else I can do. Not if I want to be able to live with myself."

She went over to the table and dropped a kiss on the crown of his head. "Don't borrow trouble, sweetie. Most of the things we worry about don't end up happening anyway."

"Yeah, I know," he said, though he didn't exactly sound convinced.

She went back to her meat loaf. "Of course, if you *do* end up having to pay, I guess settling on a figure that seems fair to both sides is going to be the hard part. Especially if you're going to try to settle out of court."

"Yeah. Out of court would be the best way, if we can manage it. I guess I do need a lawyer."

Annie cracked an egg into her meat loaf mixture and then added milk. "Maybe not quite yet, honey."

"Well, I could check with a lawyer to see what I'm facing if the will does happen to be genuine. And if it's recovered. I can brace myself for what might happen."

She gave him a little smile. "Maybe the will isn't gone for good. I hate to see you worried about something that hasn't been proven genuine in the first place. Let's see what we can find out before you start giving away what you've worked for all your life."

His smile was a little more convincing this time. "That's a good idea."

"Besides, if Bonds does know something about the will, or if he suspects that for some reason, you have something that belongs to him, why hasn't he slapped you with a lawsuit before now?"

"I don't know." Ian crossed his arms over his chest. "From what he just said to me, it sounds as if he might have one in the works."

Annie thought for a moment. "But … weren't you having trouble with him before my purse was snatched?"

"Hmmm. I guess you're right, though it got *really* bad afterward."

"And if he does have the will, why hasn't he done something about having it authenticated? From what you say, he seems mad enough to want to stir up things."

"Yeah, he does." Ian frowned. "Maybe he is afraid to bring up the will since that would implicate him in the theft."

Annie shook her head. "Tell me what he looks like again."

"Big, burly guy. Mountain-man type, beard and all."

"Well, he couldn't have been the one who took my purse." Annie gave her meat loaf a last good stirring and then pressed it into her loaf pan. "I'm not saying he couldn't have paid someone to do it, but there's no way a man of that description was the one who stole my purse."

"And there's the little problem about how your purse snatcher even knew you had that will in the first place. You're really, really, really sure you didn't mention it to anyone?"

"Really, really, really."

There was a flurry of scampering feet above them and the sound of childish laughter, and Ian and Annie looked at each other.

"Annie, you don't suppose—"

"I don't ... well, obviously the twins know about the will. They were with me when I found it in the purse lining. But really, they didn't even know what a will is. And I don't think I ever told them whose it was. I can't possibly see how they could have told anyone anything. And who would they have told? Not anyone who would have had an interest in either will."

"I'm sure you're right," he said, and then he gave her a half-pleading little grin. "Do you think we could ask them anyway?"

With a chuckle, Annie rinsed her hands and went to the foot of the stairs. "John? Joanna? Would you both come here for a minute, please?"

"Coming, Grammy!" Joanna piped.

"And please don't run on the stairs," Annie reminded them.

With a not-quite-running clatter, Joanna hurried down. John was slower to come, but soon Annie had them both sitting at the kitchen table again.

"Hey there." Ian grinned at the twins. "Sorry to interrupt whatever you were doing."

"We were building a castle out of boxes," Joanna explained. "But the lion kept knocking them down."

"Oh, I see. You have a lion now, do you?"

Joanna giggled, her eyes sparkling as if they shared a secret. "It was really only Boots, but she kept trying to jump into the top one so she could go to sleep in it, and then they all fell over."

Annie laughed, and Ian gave her a wink.

"And I suppose now it's up to you to fortify the castle walls, High King Peter?" Ian asked John.

"Yeah," John said, not looking at him, and then he turned to Annie. "Did you want to ask us something, Grammy?"

Annie gave Ian an apologetic glance and then turned again to the children. "Remember when we found that paper in the lining of that purse a couple of weeks ago?"

"That will thing?" Joanna asked. "I remember."

John nodded. "I do too."

"That's right," Annie said. "Now I want you to think very hard about this, OK? I need to know if you talked to anybody about that will. Anybody at all."

"I didn't," John said. "Can I go now?"

Annie pursed her lips. "In just a minute, John. You're sure you didn't say anything to anybody about finding it?"

He shook his head, but Joanna looked at her, big eyes round and guilty.

"Did you say something to somebody, honey?" Annie asked her. "It's OK. You're not in trouble. I just need to know who you told."

"I told Emily we found an old paper in that purse lining. She wanted to know if it was a love letter or a treasure map, but I told her it wasn't."

"And you didn't say anything else about it?"

"I told her the purse was pretty. That was at her birthday party."

Annie smiled and hugged her. "That's all right. Anybody else?"

Looking relieved, Joanna smiled a little and then wrinkled her forehead in thought. "I asked Miss Alice if she had a will. She said she did and asked me why I wanted to know, so I told her we found an old one."

"Did you tell her whose will it was, Joanna?" Ian asked, leaning down a little to have his eyes level with hers.

Joanna shook her head, ponytails swinging. "I just told her it was old. I don't know who made it."

He gave her an encouraging smile. "That's all right. Do you think you said anything to anybody else?"

Again she shook her head. "I don't think so."

"OK," Annie said. "I want you both to do me a favor and not mention anything about finding the will or about me looking for papers or anything else. Understand?"

The twins both nodded.

"Not to anybody, right?"

Again the children both nodded.

"All right," Annie said. "John, you can go back to building your castle. Joanna and I will feed the lion, and then I'll finish making supper."

John hurried back upstairs, and Joanna went to the pantry for the cat food.

"How about excusing us for just a minute?" Annie asked Ian quietly. "I'll see if Joanna can tell me anything about what's going on with John."

"Sure. I'll, uh, see if I can find Boots and tell her dinner is ready."

He went into the living room, and Annie went to the pantry to help Joanna.

"Not too much," she said as Joanna poured dry food into Boots's bowl. "She'll be too chubby to get upstairs."

Joanna laughed and closed up the bag. "She's already kind of chubby."

Annie helped her put the bag back into the pantry, and then she sat down at the table and pulled Joanna close to her.

"Tell me something, honey. Is John unhappy here?"

Joanna frowned. "He has been kind of grouchy. Not all the time."

"Do you think he misses your mom and dad?"

Joanna shrugged. "I don't think so. He didn't say he did, and usually he does."

"Did he tell you anything is bothering him?"

Again Joanna shrugged. "Nope."

"All right, honey." Annie stood up. "You go on and play, and I'll call you when dinner's ready."

"OK, Grammy."

Joanna kissed Annie's cheek and scampered off. As soon

as she was gone, Ian came back into the kitchen with Boots in his arms.

"How did it go?" he asked, putting the cat down by her bowl and then sitting down at the table.

"Joanna's as clueless as I am, I'm afraid. At least he's not homesick."

"I guess that's good. And at least you know neither of them said anything to anyone about your investigation."

Annie nodded. "They didn't talk to anyone who'd care, and they don't even know who wrote the will or who might have benefited from it."

"Hmmm." Ian drummed his fingers on the tabletop, thinking. "But *somebody* knew. The purse snatching wasn't random. The guy wanted the will. How could he have known? Think for a minute, Annie. Did anybody at all know you were researching records or looking into my family history?"

"Well, Grace Emory at the library knows I was looking at the microfilm of old newspapers, but I didn't tell her what I was looking for. I found that article where the Mayfields died in that car accident and Paul Butler's obituary and the article about Robert Mayfield saying he didn't think his grandfather died of natural causes and the whole exhumation thing. That was about all. But Grace wasn't in there with me. I asked her advice on finding some of it, but she couldn't have known what I was looking for. And please—it's Grace—you know?"

"Yeah. Ummm ... anybody else?"

She considered for another minute. "I told everybody at Mary Beth's that I'm doing some research about some papers I found, but nothing specific. No names. No dates.

How anybody could get anything from that, I don't know. There's just nobody."

"There's *somebody*, Annie."

There was a sudden realization in Ian's eyes, and Annie wrinkled her forehead.

"Who?"

"Remember when you were telling me that the woman at the courthouse was away from her desk when you came back inside after your purse was stolen?"

"Yes, but I told you, it couldn't have been—"

"Maybe she couldn't have taken your purse, but think about it. She knew exactly what records you were looking at. Deed records for the timberland and the mill. Probate records for Paul Butler and the Mayfields."

"But how would she have known about the will that hadn't been probated?"

"Did you ever take it out in front of her? Maybe to compare the two wills? To check the date? Anything like that?"

Annie bit her lip, thinking hard. "Uh, I can't really remember. I suppose I might have. But why would she care? She has to have people asking for old records all the time. Why would she care about these in particular? I mean, she has access to the old records herself. She wouldn't need to steal those. And what good would it do her?"

"I don't know. Maybe it is a little farfetched to suspect her. We'll just have to keep thinking." With a grin, he pulled Annie around to face him and put his arms around her. "I'll take you up on dinner, though, if you're still offering."

She beamed at him. "How would you feel about setting the table?"

"That is definitely something I can do."

They all had just sat down to dinner when Ian's cellphone buzzed.

"Sorry about that, Annie," he said. "I meant to turn it off before we sat down." Frowning, he reached down to his belt, pulled the phone from its holster and glanced at the caller ID. "It's the mill."

Ian clicked the cellphone. "Hello?" He mouthed "Max Austin" to Annie. "Max. Yeah. What is it now?" As he listened, Ian's jaw tightened and his eyes narrowed. "Someone did *what*? Yeah. OK. I'm on my way."

He hung up the phone and took a deep breath.

Annie put one hand on his arm. "What is it?"

"Looks like somebody set fire to the warehouse. I'm sorry, Annie, but I have to get down there right now."

Annie glanced at the twins. "I want to go with you. I'll see if I can get Alice to come over and watch things here."

"No. I don't want to upset everybody's dinner. It's all right. There's probably not much to see, as usual. Besides, I really need to get going right away."

"Let me just call Alice and see. You know she can be here in two minutes. I'd really like to be with you."

Ian threw up his hands. "OK. Call her. But if she can't come right now, I'm going to just have to go by myself. All right?"

"All right."

Two minutes later, Alice was on the front porch.

"Thanks for doing this again, Alice," Annie said, hugging her. "I'm so sorry to impose on you. There's meat loaf and veggies on the table. Help yourself."

"OK, thanks." Alice looked at Ian. "It's getting serious, isn't it?"

"I'm afraid it might be," Ian admitted. "Thanks for coming over. You're a great help. Come on, Annie. We really need to hurry."

~15~

Soon Ian and Annie were pulling up to the big metal building that warehoused the milled lumber. Inside, a smoking, half-burned stack of four-by-fours sat in the middle of a pool of water and white foam. But other than that, the damage didn't seem too bad.

Max Austin turned from inspecting some water-damaged sheets of plywood. "Ian. You made good time."

"Yeah. So what happened?"

Max shrugged. "I happened to be out here checking an order, when these four-by-fours suddenly started smoking and then burst into flames."

"Did you call the fire department?"

"Actually, no. Since it had just started, I grabbed the hose, and Tim got the fire extinguisher. We got it out. I thought I'd better wet down everything around it."

"Yeah, probably a good idea. Is Tim all right?"

"Well—"

"Hey, Ian." Tim grinned at him as he wiped foam out of his hair with a towel. "Pretty, huh?"

"Yeah." Ian looked him up and down. "What happened to you?"

Tim gave him a sheepish little grin. "I had the fire extinguisher turned the wrong way."

Ian shook his head, finally cracking a smile. "I guess you won't make that mistake twice."

Tim laughed.

"Are you all right?" Annie asked.

"Oh, yeah. I just need a good shower. Sorry about all the mess though, Ian. Guess it could have been worse."

"I guess." Ian sighed and looked around at the wood damaged by water and foam and smoke. "I guess the whole warehouse could have gone up. Did you say you didn't call the fire department, Max?"

Max frowned. "No, not since we got it all put out."

Ian nodded, tight-lipped again. "Better give them a call—and the sheriff's office. Arson is something they take pretty seriously."

Tim twisted the corner of the towel into his ear. "But I don't know how it could be arson. I didn't see anybody but Max around those four-by-fours when the fire broke out. Maybe it was just an accident. Somebody tossed a cigarette out or something."

Annie walked around the still-smoldering pile of wood. "With everything else that's been going on here, it would be a pretty amazing coincidence if this was just an accident."

"Yeah," Tim said. "I guess you must be right. But I sure haven't seen anybody around the warehouse who wasn't supposed to be here. Have you, Max?"

Max shook his head. "If you want, Ian, I'll go ahead and call the fire department and the sheriff."

"Yeah." Ian studied the burnt lumber. "And tell everybody to stay away from this area until after the police and firemen say it's clear."

Without touching anything, Annie inspected the charred ends of the four-by-fours and then the ashes from the portion that had burned. "Ian?"

Ian came over to her. "Did you find something? I don't know how the fire department is going to tell much of anything from a bunch of wet ashes and fire-retardant foam."

"Isn't this supposed to be a no-smoking building?"

Ian nodded.

"Then what's this doing here?" Annie pointed to a sodden cigarette butt barely visible under a stack of plywood sheets.

Max and Tim both came over to look.

"Maybe it was an accident after all," Max said. "Could be somebody was out here catching a smoke and dropped the cigarette when somebody else came by, afraid he'd get caught."

Tim nodded in agreement. "Must have been."

"I'll find out who all was working in here today," Max said. "We had a crew loading up that Marchfield order." Max looked at Ian. "Do you still want me to call the police and the fire department?"

Annie gave him a subtle nod, and Ian nodded to Max.

"I think you'd better. This whole thing doesn't look right."

"OK. I'll call them right now."

Max hurried back toward the office, and Tim looked at Annie.

"It's just a cigarette butt," he said. "Doesn't mean much, does it? Except that someone was smoking in here who shouldn't have been."

"Maybe," Annie said, "but I just don't think so. If that is what started the fire, then why is it over here by the plywood sheets and not over there by the four-by-fours?"

Ian frowned. "Right."

"And why is this mark here?"

Annie pointed to where the foam was smeared, as if something had been slid out of it toward the stack of plywood.

"And," she added, "why is there foam on the cigarette butt and not anywhere else over here? It couldn't have been here until just now."

Ian's eyes sparked with anger. "Tim, who all was in here when you and Max were putting out the fire?"

"I'm not sure, Ian. Several of the guys were out here. Jenkins, Murray, that new guy Flynn. I'm not sure who else."

"OK, get them out here. Anybody who was in the lot once you brought the fire extinguisher out, get him out here."

"Right."

Tim darted off, and Annie took Ian's arm.

"What are you going to do?"

Ian shrugged. "I'm not exactly sure. I guess just look the guys over and see if anything seems funny about any of them. If somebody moved that cigarette butt away from where the fire started, then he ought to have some of that foam on him somewhere."

"Unless he's already wiped it all off."

"Well, it won't hurt to look."

A few minutes later, Tim had rounded up several of the men. Ian and Annie looked them over, especially their shoes.

"What's this all about, Ian?" asked a tall, bearded man Annie remembered was Murray.

"You were all in the warehouse when the fire broke out, right?"

The men nodded, murmuring their assent.

"All of you," Ian confirmed. "Do any of you remember seeing anybody around at that time who's not here right now?"

"Max Austin," said another man, and several of them agreed.

"Right," Ian said. "He's calling the police and the fire department. Anybody else?"

The men conferred briefly, and then Murray spoke for them. "I think we're it."

"All right," Ian said, giving them all a penetrating look. "How many of you smoke?"

Several raised their hands. A few of those looked puzzled, a couple of them defiant. Annie checked their shoes again.

"Hey, Flynn, put your hand up, man." Murray elbowed the lanky, dark-haired young man standing next to him. "You bummed a cigarette from me not even two hours ago."

The one called Flynn ducked his head and then half-heartedly lifted his hand. Ian narrowed his eyes.

"So you are a smoker, Flynn?"

"Yes, Mr. Butler."

Ian nodded. "And were you smoking in here this afternoon?"

Flynn's head dropped lower. "Yes, sir, I was."

"You do know we don't let anyone smoke in here. For obvious reasons."

"Yes, sir, I do know that." Flynn looked up at him, dark eyes pleading. "Look, I'm really sorry, Mr. Butler. I just really needed a smoke, and I had a long time until my next break. I didn't think it would hurt anything if I ducked out of sight and lit up. I swear I thought I had put it out. I mean, I really ground it out with my boot. Then, after the fire broke out, and Mr. Austin and Tim pretty much got it under control, I saw that stupid butt there by the four-by-fours. I, um…"

"You what?" Ian insisted.

"Well, I kinda pushed it out of the way. I swear, Mr. Butler, I don't even know how it got over there in the first place. I was over by the one-inch boards. I don't know if somebody coming by accidentally kicked it over by the four-by-fours, or when we had the doors open to load the truck, if the wind might have blown it over there. I just don't know. I'm really sorry."

Annie couldn't help feeling sorry for the young man. He did have just a few flecks of the fire-retardant foam still on the tip of his work boot. Maybe this was just due to a careless accident after all.

Ian paced for a moment, jaw clenched, and then he turned back to the men. "Any of the rest of you have anything to say about this? Did any of you see anything that would make this seem deliberate?"

All the men shook their heads.

"I don't guess you've figured out who's been stirring things up here, have you?" Murray asked.

"Not yet." Ian sighed. "OK, you guys get back to work."

"I really am sorry, Mr. Butler," Flynn said.

Ian shook his head. "Accidents happen. I guess I'm a little on edge with everything that's been going on around here."

"You can take the damage out of my pay," the young man offered, and Ian gave him a reluctant grin.

"This one's on me. But next time, you're out of here. Deal?"

"Yeah. Deal." Flynn turned, stopped, and then turned back. "Uh, thanks, Mr. Butler."

"Yeah, yeah—get back to work."

When all the men were gone, Annie slipped her arm around Ian's waist. "Pushover."

Ian shrugged. "He's just a kid. I made my share of 'I just wasn't thinking' mistakes at his age." He gave her a wink. "Can't say I don't make my fair share still."

"Don't we all." She laughed and then sobered. "So what did you think of his story?"

"I think he's telling the truth."

She nodded. "I do too. But I'm not sure it could have started that fire if he dropped it over by the plywood. I know it's been pretty dry lately. Where did he say he'd put out his cigarette?"

"He said he was by the one-inch boards."

They walked over to where the one-inch boards were stacked.

"What are you looking for?" Ian asked.

Annie shook her head. "I'm not sure yet. I'm just not really satisfied that that cigarette could have gotten over to those four-by-fours without some help."

Hands braced on her knees, she bent over to look closer at the cement floor next to the pallet on which the one-inch boards were stacked. Then she looked up at Ian, smiling.

"I thought that might be the case."

He wrinkled his forehead and bent down too. "What?"

"I don't want to touch anything until the police or fire department get here, but see that right there? Right under the corner of the pallet."

He grinned. "One little cigarette butt."

"Uh-huh. Over here where young Mr. Flynn was

actually smoking, and pretty much ground into the cement. Which means ...?"

"Which means," Ian said, "there was someone else smoking in here too."

"Or someone set that fire to go off when he had a good alibi."

Ian frowned. "What do you mean?"

"It's an old trick, isn't it? You light a cigarette and put the other end in a book of matches that's next to something that will catch fire easily. You have as long as it takes the cigarette to burn to get out of the area. Or if you need more time, you make a line of cigarettes and let them burn." Annie walked back toward the foam-covered section of the floor. "I bet the arson investigator will find something like that under the ashes."

Ian followed her, studying the burned area. "So, instead of questioning anyone who was here when the fire started, we should be wondering about someone who particularly *wasn't* here?" He laughed faintly. "That's a lot of folks."

"Yeah." She folded her arms, thinking. "Did any of your men take time off this afternoon? Vacation? Doctor's appointment? Sick leave? Or did you have anybody come in here earlier today who isn't usually around?"

"I'll have to ask Max. He'd know."

Annie nodded, looking over his shoulder. "There he is."

"I talked to the sheriff's office and the fire department," Max said. "Both said they'd send somebody out as soon as they could."

"Great." Ian clasped Max's shoulder. "Tell me something. Do we have any of the crew out today? For anything?"

Max shrugged. "Calder's wife's having their baby. He got called out at about a quarter of ten this morning. Stanley's with his family in Colorado since last week. Those are the only two. Why?"

"Just trying to figure out who's been around. Any unexpected guests that you know of? Visitors? Delivery people?"

Max shook his head. "Not that I ever saw. Want me to ask around?"

"Yeah, if you would."

"Right away."

~ 16 ~

"So what happened?" Alice asked, wide-eyed, when Annie and Ian got back to Grey Gables.

"Are the twins asleep already?" Annie asked, looking around the living room.

There was a nearly empty bowl of popcorn and a stack of children's DVDs on the floor next to a couple of big pillows and Petunia, the giant stuffed bear.

"They conked out right before you got here." Alice smiled. "I managed to get Joanna into bed without waking her up, but John told me he wasn't sleepy. He walked up on his own. Then he passed out."

"Good." Annie tossed the pillows onto a chair. "Sorry we were gone so long."

"So what happened?" Alice asked again. "Was there a lot of damage?"

Ian sighed. "Why don't we sit down? It's been quite a day."

Once they were settled on the couch, Alice looked at them expectantly. "Well?"

"We don't know a lot yet," Ian said. "The arson investigator found some evidence that it was arson and definitely not just a careless accident. Someone used a cigarette as a way to set the fire after he had gone. The investigator questioned some of the men, and so did the police, but they say it's pretty early on for them to come to any conclusions."

Alice gave him a sympathetic smile. "How bad was the damage?"

"Could have been worse," Ian admitted. "The fire got part of a stack of four-by-fours, but the worst part was from water and the fire extinguisher."

Annie nodded. "The investigator said the guys did a good job of putting the fire out before it really had a chance to get going. Otherwise, with all that lumber, it could have been a pretty big blaze."

"And nobody was hurt, I hope," Alice said.

"No." Ian glanced at Annie and then chuckled. "Tim had a run-in with the fire extinguisher, but that's about it."

Alice laughed. "I'm glad it wasn't any worse than that. What about you, Annie? Got any ideas on who did it?"

"No." Annie exhaled heavily and then frowned. "I guess, since the fire was set with an incendiary device with a time delay, the only people we can rule out are the ones who were actually there when it started."

"Yeah," Ian said. "So, all that's left to suspect is the population of the world minus about six. That narrows it right down."

Alice frowned, thinking. "I'm not so sure. It could be it was someone who was there—someone who's around a lot and who thought being there when the fire broke out would actually *remove* him from suspicion."

"Right," Ian said. "Before now, it could have been anybody. Things mostly happened at night when there was nobody around. But this had to have been set up no more than an hour or so before Max noticed the smoke. So if it's not somebody who works for me, it's somebody who managed to sneak into the warehouse without anyone noticing."

"I suppose you've known everybody at the mill for a long time, huh?" Alice asked.

Ian nodded. "Most of them."

"What about the new guy?" Annie lifted one eyebrow. "Flynn, is it?"

"Yeah," Ian said. "He seemed like he was telling the truth, but I guess we can't rule him out. Maybe Cliff Bonds got him to come work for me so he could sabotage things."

Alice frowned. "Cliff Bonds? How does he fit into all this?"

Briefly, Annie explained the connection between Bonds and Ian and some of the suspicions they had.

"I didn't know he had anything to do with your family, Ian," Alice said. "This could be a big deal."

Annie nodded. "Very big. And, no, we can't rule Bonds out. But if he wants the mill property, what good does it do for him to sabotage things? Wouldn't he just be devaluing something he thinks ought to be his?"

"Yeah," Ian said. "Maybe."

"Whoever is doing this seems angry. Spiteful. Remember that broken brick we found the night the office windows were broken? The one that said 'justice'?"

Ian nodded, his mouth grim. "And Cliff sure seemed angry when I talked to him last."

"It still seems counterproductive," Annie said. "And I don't know why Cliff would be mad at you anyway. Not you personally. You didn't know any more about the new will than he did. You certainly didn't set out to cheat him out of anything."

"No. Like I've said before, he and I had a good working relationship until recently. It's like somebody has him all stirred up."

Alice looked at Annie and Ian. "You know, maybe you ought to figure out who has a grudge against you personally, Ian. Maybe it doesn't really have anything to do with the mill at all."

Annie nodded. "You might be absolutely right. That would explain all the incidents that happened before we even knew there was this new will."

"OK, maybe that's true. But who would it be?" Ian shrugged. "I can't think of anybody who'd have a reason to have it in for me."

"It's not always a rational thing," Annie told him, giving his hand a squeeze. "Have you had a run-in with anyone on Stony Point business lately in your capacity as mayor? Fired anyone? Turned down a job application? Upset a customer?"

"Hmmm. I guess we've had a lot of upset customers since this has been going on. I think I've smoothed most everything over, but I don't know. There is one place that says they're not buying from us again. Ever. But that business has been a customer for decades. I'm hoping things will cool off with them. As far as I know, the mayor's office has been pretty quiet. I still can't help Mrs. Adams with the rats in her garage, but I don't think she has it in for me because of that. I've lost my temper a time or two with an employee."

"Tim?" Alice asked.

Ian chuckled. "Yeah, he does get a little careless sometimes, but we've worked things out all right. I haven't fired anybody since fall of last year, if I remember right."

Annie raised one eyebrow. "Any chance that person is behind all this?"

"Not unless he can stir up trouble all the way from

Oregon," Ian told her. "He took a job out there when I terminated him. He moved his family and everything. I don't think he even has relatives in the state now."

"Hmmm."

"I hired Flynn about a month ago."

Annie frowned. "Was that before or after the trouble started?"

"Let me see. I think it was about the same time. It may be that things started happening a few days afterward."

"But not before."

Ian shook his head. "Not before. He was there when we had the incident with the spray paint, and that was when this all started."

"Spray paint?" Alice asked.

Ian sighed. "Yeah, black and red spray paint on the outside of the warehouse."

"I never heard anything about that." Alice turned her glance from Annie to Ian. "What did it say?"

"Just vandalism, really. A few vulgar words, something about injustice and making things right. I don't remember now. We took pictures, and then I had it all cleaned off. It wasn't very good paint."

"And you're sure Flynn was already working for you by then?" Annie asked.

"Yeah. That's why I even brought up the incident. He's one of the guys I had clean up the mess."

"Maybe you ought to have someone keep an eye on him," Alice suggested. "Without letting him know, of course."

"Probably not a bad idea," Annie said, "but I still don't think it's him."

"Why?" Ian gave her a reluctant grin. "Women's intuition?"

"No, not that really. I just don't know what motive he would have for doing any of this. What does he stand to gain?"

"Money's always a pretty good motivator, don't you think?"

"You think someone's paying him to disrupt things at the mill?" Alice asked.

"And the logical person to be doing that would be Bonds," Annie insisted. "And, again, I don't know how it would benefit him to ruin things at the mill if he hopes it's going to be turned over to him. This has to be somebody who's angry about something. And I'd bet anything that he's too angry to let anyone get the satisfaction of doing his dirty work for him."

Ian sighed and stood up. "I guess all we can do is get a good night's sleep and see what we can find out in the morning."

"I really appreciate you coming over at the last minute, Alice," Annie said. "You're a lifesaver."

"No problem. But I'd better get back home. I have a midmorning party set up for Divine Décor, and it's all the way over in Camden. See you two later."

She hurried off, and then Ian reached out for Annie's hands and pulled her up off the couch. "I'd better go too. Thanks again for coming with me. You make everything better."

She put her arms around his neck, smiling up at him. "Everything is an awful lot."

"Well, it's true." He slipped his arms around her waist. "I could get used to having you around all the time."

Her heart beat a little faster. He wasn't going to—

"In fact," he said, looking deeply into her eyes, "I really can't imagine having to be without you at all."

He was. She dropped her eyes, swallowing hard. He was, and she didn't have a clue what to say to him. Was she ready for this? She waited and then looked up at him again. He looked a little flustered, and then he smiled wryly.

"But I guess I have to be without you at least until tomorrow."

"Ian?"

He kissed her and smiled. "It's pretty late. Call you tomorrow?"

"Sure."

They kissed again on the front porch, and then she stood watching until he was out of sight. Had he actually been about to propose? Or was that her imagination? Had she been mistaken, or had he lost his nerve? And if he finally asked, what was she going to say?

— 17 —

Thursday dawned spectacularly beautiful. The previous evening almost seemed to Annie to be a bad dream. While John went to a local baseball game with the two Chapman boys and their mother from down the street, Annie and Joanna went to buy some groceries. Afterward, seeing Ian's truck parked in front of Town Hall, Annie smiled.

"How about we go by and say hi to Mr. Ian?"

"Oh, good," Joanna said. "Can I take him some of the grapes we got?"

Annie laughed. "Sure. That would be very thoughtful, honey."

Annie pulled off a cluster of the green grapes she had just bought and put them in one of the plastic bags and gave it to her granddaughter. Then she and Joanna hurried over to the mayor's office. Mrs. Nash was on the phone as usual, but she smiled and waved them into Ian's office.

"Mr. Ian!" Joanna scampered over to Ian's side of the desk, holding up the grapes. "Look what we got. Do you want some? I like grapes best."

She stuffed a few into her mouth, grinning, and then offered Ian the bag.

"Thanks, sweetie," he said with a smile that didn't quite reach his eyes. "I'll have some in a little while."

Joanna glanced at Annie and then back at Ian. "Didn't you want us to come see you, Mr. Ian?"

He laughed and gave her a hug. "Sure I did. I've just been a little busy. But I should never get too busy to see my best girls. Now tell me what you two have been doing."

Annie watched while Joanna chattered about the groceries they had bought, and then Annie pulled out the paper and crayons that Ian kept in a drawer for her grandchildren.

"Why don't you draw Mr. Ian a picture of his dog? Then he can take it home and show it to Tartan!"

"Would he like that, Mr. Ian? I know my daddy always likes it when I draw his picture."

"I know he'd like it a lot," Ian told her. "He might like it so much he'd try to eat it."

Joanna giggled and then sat beside the desk and started coloring.

"What's wrong?" Annie asked softly, putting her arm through his.

He didn't say anything. He just took a letter from his desk and handed it to her.

The stationery was somber and professional. "Jackson E. Rogers, III, Attorney at Law." The address was in Newcastle. She read the letter over and then looked up, wide-eyed.

"This says Bonds is planning on filing an eviction suit."

"Yep." Ian's smile was grim. "If I want to stay out of court, I'm supposed to turn over the mill and the property it's on within ninety days."

"But how can they possibly ask you to do that? It's not right. Not after all the work you and your family have put into it for nearly a hundred years!"

"Well, according to the letter, he'll be filing the new will and having it probated. Which means the mill would go to Bonds."

"So somehow the will got from the man who snatched my purse and into Cliff Bonds's hands. Has anyone said how that happened?" Annie asked.

"I asked, and they said Cliff was mailed the will by an anonymous person who wanted to 'set the record straight.'"

"And the house they mention here?"

"Hmmm ... as far as I remember being told, the house they're talking about burned down sometime after World War II, and the lot was sold. I never had title to it. I never even thought about it being part of all this, but it was part of the real property that was deeded to my side of the family. I suppose Bonds could try to sue me for the value of the land."

Annie took his hand, holding it tightly. "Oh, Ian."

"I talked to the attorney I usually deal with when there's a legal issue at the mill, Calvin Wingate, but he said I needed to talk to someone who specializes in wills and probate."

"Did he give you a referral?" Annie asked.

"Yeah, a guy in Friendship. His name's Patterson, and Calvin says he's really good. Um, would you like to go with me when I talk to him? My appointment is at three tomorrow."

"I'd love to go. The twins are supposed to go see a movie with Peggy and Emily since Peggy has the day off, so the timing is perfect. You don't think it will take more than a couple of hours, do you?"

"I don't know. I don't have a lot of experience with these things. Do you think Peggy would mind if the kids played at her house until we're done? I hope we'll be through before the movie's over, but I can't promise."

"I'll ask her. I don't think she'd mind. In fact, I think we'll stop over at The Cup & Saucer on the way back to the car and ask her. If it doesn't work out, I'll let you know. Otherwise, I'll plan on going with you."

*   *   *   *

Marvin G. Patterson's office was situated at one end of a strip mall in Friendship. Ian held open the door for Annie and then followed her inside. Then they both stopped short. There was a tiny reception area with a loveseat and a chair and a meticulous-looking desk where a rather dowdy brunette sat talking on the phone. Beyond that was what had to be Patterson's "office."

Annie had never seen anything like it. The desk and the library table along the wall, every chair and the floor were piled high with papers and open folders and thick books— law books, she assumed—with more papers stuck in them in multiple places. Littered all over were business cards and phone messages and receipts and scraps torn from notepads.

"I think a grenade went off in there," Annie whispered.

Chuckling, Ian put one finger to his lips.

The secretary excused herself and put her hand over the receiver.

"Mr. Butler?"

"That's right," Ian said. "I have an appointment at three."

She smiled. "If you don't mind having a seat, Mr. Patterson will be with you in just a minute."

"Thank you."

They sat down, and Annie noticed it was about ten minutes till three. About fifteen minutes later, a lanky, balding man in a rather shiny brown suit hurried in through the front door. He carried a day planner bursting with papers and business cards. This had to be Patterson.

He pushed his comb-over back into place, and smiling, offered Ian his hand. "Mr. Butler, I presume. I'm Marv Patterson."

Ian and Annie stood up.

"Yes, sir." Ian shook his hand. "This is Annie Dawson."

"Hello." Patterson shook Annie's hand too. "Sorry to have kept you waiting. Come on back to my office."

He led them through to the other room and moved the clutter from two of the chairs so they could sit down.

"Calvin Wingate told me you have a rather unusual case." From his day planner, Patterson pulled out a form that had Ian's name and phone number handwritten at the top, and then he took a lined yellow pad and a pen out of a drawer. "Why don't you tell me about it?"

Ian told him about Annie finding the will, about it being stolen and about Bonds's strange behavior.

"I guess it all makes sense now. He believes I have something that rightfully ought to be his, Mr. Patterson."

"Call me Marv, Ian."

Ian nodded. "All right, Marv. Anyway, I have concerns about how Bonds got the new will in the first place."

"He couldn't have been the one who snatched my purse," Annie said. "He's too big. But he could have hired someone to do it."

Patterson's eyebrows raised. "So he admits it was stolen?"

"No," Ian said. "He says it was mailed to him anonymously."

"And do you believe him?"

Ian shrugged. "I'm not sure whether I do or not. I've done business with him for a lot of years. He's not the easiest guy to get along with, but he's been straight with me. Up until now, that is. And his story is so farfetched, it just might be true."

Patterson raised one eyebrow. "But?"

"But he could have hired someone to take the will. He could be behind all the vandalism at the mill too, though I'm not really sure how that would benefit him. And he just doesn't seem the type to do that kind of thing. He's more of the 'come up and punch you in the face' kind of guy, you know?"

Patterson grinned. "Well, frankly, I don't think he has much to go on in filing this suit. I don't want you to worry too much. They haven't actually filed suit, and they can't possibly do anything unless and until they do. This will is getting close to being a hundred years old. It was never probated. And during that hundred years, the mill property has been in your branch of the family. You've carried out your business there in the public eye, and you've paid taxes and otherwise made it plain that you own the place. That gives you a pretty good chance of prevailing if Bonds actually takes you to court."

Ian frowned. "But only a chance."

"Certainly. You can never guarantee how a case will turn out, but I'd say your chances are very good."

"Legally, maybe," Ian said. "But what about morally? I

mean, what if Bonds really ought to own the mill? What if his part of the family should have gotten it in the first place?"

"Well, of course, that would be something you'd have to decide for yourself. I'm just here to help you through the legal aspects of the case."

"Right. I appreciate that."

"Is there anything Ian should be doing at this point?" Annie asked. "Is there any way we can make Bonds return the will to me? However he came by it, it was stolen from me, after all."

Patterson frowned. "Of course, if he stole the will or hired someone to do that, that's a criminal offense. However, the ownership of the will itself would be a matter for the courts to decide. I can't say for certain at this point, but I would assume it would belong to whoever would benefit under the terms of the will. But honestly, after nearly a hundred years? I don't think that document means much. Your family hasn't been hiding it all these years, have they? Trying to defraud Mr. Bonds's side of the family?"

Ian chuckled. "If they were, they sure didn't tell me."

"Then I very much doubt Mr. Bonds has much of a case. He might not even find a court that would hear it if he goes as far as actually filing suit." Patterson picked up the letter Bonds's attorney had sent Ian, glancing over it again. "I don't know Mr. Rogers personally, but if he's agreeing to pursue this case for Mr. Bonds, I'd have to ask myself what he hopes to get out of it."

Ian leaned forward. "You mean—"

"I don't know the particulars," Patterson said, holding up one hand. "So I won't say anymore on that subject. But I do want to say that I don't think you need to be too worried about that will."

He stood up, offering Ian his hand again, and Ian and Annie stood too.

"I sure appreciate it, Marv." Ian shook his hand heartily. "You've taken a big load off my mind. How much do I owe you?"

"Not a thing today." Patterson smiled. "You really didn't need anything but a little information, and I was happy to give it to you. Now if either of you ends up needing a new will drawn up or any assistance with estate planning, I'd sure be happy to help you with that. And if this threatened lawsuit actually gets filed—well, I'd be happy to represent you."

"We'll definitely keep that in mind," Annie said, shaking his hand too. "Thank you."

Once they were out in the parking lot again, Annie threw her arms around Ian's neck and gave him a smacking kiss.

"Isn't that great? Even if the will *is* valid, it's way too late to enforce it."

"Yeah."

Annie's smile faded. Ian still looked troubled.

"What is it, Ian?"

He only shrugged. "Maybe I don't have to worry too much about Bonds's legal right to the mill, but again, what if he really should have it, whether or not the law says he can take it from me? What if Paul Butler meant to disinherit my side of the family and give it all to Bonds's side? I need to know if that will is valid."

"Well, wouldn't Bonds need to know that too? I mean, if he really is set on pursuing legal action, wouldn't he first get the will checked out?"

"I need to talk to him." Ian bit his lip. "I guess I can try to call him again. If he won't talk to me, at least I can leave him a message. Patterson wouldn't come out and say it, but it sounds like this Rogers either doesn't know his business, or he's just trying to get as much money as possible from Bonds for a lawsuit he knows he can't win."

"You mean Rogers works for 'Dewey, Cheatem & Howe.'"

Ian chuckled. "After all that's happened, maybe I should just let Bonds find that out for himself."

Annie shook her head. "I know you better than that. Maybe Bonds deserves it, but I know you wouldn't let that happen without at least trying to warn him."

Again he shrugged. "Gotta live with myself, you know."

She hugged him once more. "Did I ever tell you what a good man you are?"

"You may have mentioned something along those lines once or twice." He opened the car door for her. "Now, how about we go pick up the twins, and I'll take you all out for dinner?"

"You spoil us all, you know."

He winked at her. "I try my best."

— 18 —

*I*an listened to the phone ring. One. Two. Three. Four. Then there was a click. "Leave a message, and I'll get back to you." Cliff Bonds's gravelly voice was followed by a piercing beep.

Ian took a deep breath. "Hey, Cliff, this is Ian Butler. I just wanted you to know that I went to see an attorney today about the letter your attorney sent me. My attorney says that because it's been so long since the will you have was written, even if it's valid, it's way too late to probate it. He doesn't think a court is even likely to hear your case. I'm not saying you can't pursue it if you want to, but I don't think it's going to do you any good. I don't know what you're paying that lawyer of yours, but you might want to get a second opinion before you pay him too much more. The other thing is, I'd really like you to get that will looked over. I want to know whether or not it's the real thing. If not, well, no harm done. But if it is—if your side of the family should have gotten the mill and not mine—I want to know it. Even if the law can't do anything about it, I want to do what's right. If that will is genuine, I'd want to do something to—"

There was a click and a clatter on the other end of the line. "Ian. Ian? Are you there?"

"I'm here, Cliff. I guess you heard what I called about."

For a long moment there was only silence. Then Bonds cleared his throat.

"I, uh—yeah, I did. What exactly are you trying to pull?"

Ian exhaled heavily. "I'm not trying to pull anything. Come on, Cliff. We've had business dealings for what? Twenty? Twenty-five years? When have I ever tried to pull something over on you?"

"All right," Bonds admitted. "Maybe you haven't. But this is big. Really big. I mean, we're talking your whole business, right? I'd probably try whatever I could to keep it if I were in your shoes."

"Maybe so, Cliff. But I want to do what's right here. Even if your side of the family should have inherited everything, there's no way the law would just make me turn the mill over to you. My side of the family has built that business up for nearly a hundred years. The best you could expect is some kind of compensation."

"Yeah, well, it would be fairly substantial, I'm sure. My lawyer tells me the value of the property at the time my family should have inherited it with compound interest all these years is pretty huge."

Ian chuckled grimly. "Yeah, I suppose it would be. I do have a question for you though."

"Yeah?"

"Where'd you find this lawyer you're working with? I thought you used 'Preston, Porter & Marks'?"

"I do."

"Then why didn't you ask them about this?"

"I did, in fact," Bonds said. "I talked to Allen Preston himself. He said this kind of thing isn't their specialty and told me I needed to get someone who does wills and probate."

"And they recommended this Rogers guy?"

"Well, uh … not exactly. I looked him up myself."

Ian sighed. "And he told you what you wanted to hear, so you didn't look any further."

"Look, Ian—"

"Don't get mad, Cliff. I didn't call you to rile you up. I just hoped we could have a reasonable discussion about all this. As I said, if you're due something because Paul Butler meant your side of the family to have the mill, then I want to do what I can to make it right with you—because it's the right thing to do, not because I was forced to."

Bonds was silent for a moment. "Listen, Ian, I don't know a lot of guys who'd do that. You'll have to forgive me for being a little skeptical."

Ian chuckled. "Fair enough. But I also don't want you to lose a lot of money chasing a lawsuit that you can never win."

"Now I get it. You want to sweet-talk me into settling for nothing. Well, you can forget that."

"Come on, Cliff—"

"Rogers says that we have a will that revokes all previous ones. The one that was probated is previous. It's as simple as that. He says we can win this."

"Cliff, I'm not trying to talk you into or out of anything, OK? If you want to pay this Rogers guy a couple of hundred dollars an hour to work on a case that the court's not even going to hear, that's up to you. I just felt like it was my responsibility to tell you what I found out."

"OK, you told me."

Ian shook his head at the stubbornness in Bonds's voice. "Fine. I'm just suggesting you get a second opinion about it, and that you get that will authenticated. Even if you did have a case, it all falls apart if that will's a fake."

"Why would it be fake, huh? Tell me that."

"Why would it be hidden all this time? And why would somebody steal it and send it to you? I don't know the answer to any of that yet. I'm just saying you could save yourself a lot of money and trouble if you'd just get it checked out."

Bonds scoffed. "Fine. You've done your Boy Scout duty. I'm duly cautioned."

Ian clenched his jaw. "Great. I guess that's all I had to say."

"Great. Then thanks for calling."

The next thing Ian heard was a click and a dial tone. He sighed and hung up. At least he had done his best to do what was right.

*   *   *   *

"Feel like a little company?"

Ian looked up to see Annie standing in the door of his office at Town Hall. He smiled and stood up to hug her. "Always. As long as it's you."

"I just dropped the twins off at play practice, and I have a few minutes before I have to go to the Hook and Needle Club meeting over at A Stitch in Time."

"The twins have play practice?"

"Well, just a little skit really. Their Sunday School class is doing it for the church this week. Joanna is Noah's wife and John is one of the lions. They each have a little song to do too."

"That'll be cute."

"Anyway, I don't have to get to Mary Beth's for a little while yet, and I thought I'd check on you. You were pretty quiet after church on Sunday, and I didn't hear from you yesterday. Everything OK?"

"Yeah, same as usual." He pulled up a chair for her and then sat back in his own. "Haven't had any more incidents at the mill, thank goodness. I'm just trying to keep things together until I hear something about this lawsuit. I guess the waiting's the hardest part."

"I don't suppose you've heard anything from Mr. Bonds, huh?"

Ian shook his head. "After I talked to him on Friday, I got the impression that he was going to go ahead with the suit no matter what."

The phone on Ian's desk buzzed, and he excused himself to answer it. "Yes, Charlotte?"

"Cliff Bonds is calling for you," she said.

"Uh, OK. Yeah, put him through." Ian looked at Annie, eyebrows raised, and then put Bonds on speaker-phone. "Cliff? This is a surprise. I am in my office with Annie Dawson. Since the will you have was taken from her stolen purse, I thought it would be good for her to hear what you have to say today, so I have you on my speaker-phone. What can I do for you?"

For a moment there was only silence on the other end of the line, and then Bonds cleared his throat. "I, uh, I did a lot of thinking about what you told me the other day, Ian. About getting a second opinion about the case and all that."

"Oh, really?"

"Yeah. I got one. A second opinion, I mean. And a third. Both of them said I didn't have much of a chance in pursuing an unprobated hundred-year-old will."

Ian let out a silent sigh of relief. *Thank God.*

"Well, I can't exactly say I'm sorry," Ian told him, "but I'm glad you found out now, before you blew a bunch of money on a worthless lawsuit."

Ian looked at Annie who was grinning at him.

"Yeah," said Bonds. "I'm going to have a good long discussion with my attorney about wasting my money too."

He didn't say anything else, though Ian could tell he wanted to.

"I was serious about doing something to compensate you if that will is valid," Ian told him. "You ought to get it checked out."

Bonds laughed sheepishly. "Yeah, well, that's the other thing. I did get it checked out. They said the paper and the ink are definitely from about 1920. The sort of typewriter that was used fits into that time period too. And the signatures of the witnesses are authentic."

Ian waited. He could hear a "but" in Bonds's voice.

"But," Bonds said finally, "it's their opinion that the old man's signature was traced off the will that *was* probated. The one that split the properties between your side of the family and mine."

"The valid will."

Bonds let out a long breath. "Yeah."

Ian looked again at Annie, shaking his head and smiling in amazement. "So you're telling me Paul Butler's signature on the 1920 will is a forgery?"

"Exactly," Cliff said. "Seems I've hassled you for no reason and made a pretty big fool of myself in the process. All I can do is drop the suit and say I'm sorry."

"No hard feelings," Ian said. "Actually, I'm feeling so happy to hear all this, there's no way I could be mad. But can I ask you something, Cliff?"

"Sure. Go ahead."

"Way before that will was stolen," Ian said, "you were mad about something. Why? If you didn't even know there was a will until a week or more ago, why were you taking it out on me and my mill?"

"I started getting anonymous messages saying you had been ripping me off for years. I guess I got the first one—I don't know—maybe sometime in May. I just tossed them at first. We hadn't had any problems to speak of. Nothing we couldn't get straightened out. But then things really started happening. We didn't get paid on time, or we only got partial payments, or your people would call up asking where an order was that we didn't ever have record of receiving. It was just some things here and there, and your company always had some answer for the mix-ups on your end of things. But by then those notes started making sense to me."

"So then you started giving me a hard time about my orders and not returning calls and all that, right?"

"Yeah." Bonds sounded more than a little embarrassed. "I've been getting these notes for a while now, saying there was proof the mill should belong to me and not you. By then I was hopping mad and pretty much ready to do whatever it took to get back at you. It seems kind of silly now."

Ian chuckled. "You could have just come and talked to me, you know."

"Yeah. Would have saved us both a lot of trouble."

"And you don't know who sent you those notes? Or the will?"

"Not a clue. I wish I did. I'd punch that guy right in the nose."

Ian hesitated for a moment. "Do you mind if I have a look at them? I'd sure like to know what's going on, and it seems pretty likely that whoever sent them is behind all the other things going on around the mill."

"What other things?"

"Mainly vandalism. Broken windows, a fire rigged in the warehouse, some fence cut, lots of mechanical and computer breakdowns. Stuff like you were describing between my company and yours. So, do you mind me stopping by later today and looking at those notes? Maybe there's something—"

"Um, yeah, sure. I don't know what good they'll do you. There's not much to them. I thought about calling the police about them, but they're not threatening or anything. I don't know if sending something like this, even if it's all lies, is against the law."

"I'd really like to see anyway."

Bonds laughed softly. "Sure. I'll give you the will too. Come by the office anytime, and you can pick it all up. And I promise I won't say I'm out when I'm not."

"Sounds fair enough," Ian said, chuckling too. "I have to go out to the mill this afternoon, so I'll stop by your place on my way home if that's all right."

"Yeah. And, Ian—no hard feelings, huh?"

"Water under the bridge, Cliff. Don't worry about it. See you this afternoon."

Ian hung up the phone and then sat for a moment just staring at it. "I—I don't know what to say."

"The will's a forgery?" Annie clapped her hands together, eyes dancing. "It's a miracle. A true miracle."

"It is." He let out a taut breath, and then he grinned at her. "It sure is."

"So who is our mystery troublemaker?" Annie asked. "Who's been stirring up trouble between you and Cliff?" She came around to his side of the desk and put her arms around him. "I have to go to my meeting now, but I sure would like to see whatever you get from Bonds."

"I'll drop by on my way back home this afternoon. How's that?"

"That's just perfect. Umm ... is it OK if I tell everybody at Mary Beth's what's been going on now?"

Ian laughed. "Sure. Not that we know who's been stirring up trouble, but at least we know the mill is rightfully mine, and I don't have any upcoming lawsuits, so you can tell them all about your investigation. I know you've been dying to tell them the story."

Annie leaned down and kissed him. "I have, but when I tell it, I'll make sure you're the hero."

*   *   *   *

By the time Annie finished telling everyone at the Hook and Needle Club about finding the will and everything that had happened since, the only sound was the swift clicking of Stella's knitting needles.

"Wow," Gwen said finally. "What a story. I'm glad everything about Ian's inheritance is all right."

"Me too," Kate said with a shake of her head. "But what about everything that's been going on out at the mill? You still don't know who's behind that."

Peggy nodded. "Wally said it was quite a mess out there when he went to replace those windows."

"Well, I knew you and Alice were up to something," Mary Beth said, chuckling as she went back to the order of quilting threads she was checking in. "Be careful, Annie. Who knows what the person behind all this is going to do next!"

"Don't worry," Annie said. "I will be. And he's not going to be able to hide forever. Ian is supposed to go pick up the anonymous letters Cliff Bonds got. Maybe there will be something there that gives our troublemaker away."

~ 19 ~

Annie hurried to the door as soon as she heard Ian's knock.

"Good afternoon, ma'am." He bowed slightly and then held up a manila envelope. "Could I interest you in a little mystery fodder?"

She grinned at him. "Is that what I think it is?"

"I haven't had a chance to look at what's inside yet, but Cliff said it's the forged will and those notes he got. Well, it's some of them anyway. He said he threw away the first few, and I'm afraid he didn't keep the envelopes for most of them, but he said there are some."

She took the envelope from him and pulled him down the central hall of Grey Gables and into the kitchen behind her. "We can spread it all out on the table and see what there is."

"Great."

They sat down, and Annie opened the envelope and took out several sheets of paper and some smaller envelopes. The envelopes were addressed to Bonds at his office in plain, unpunctuated block letters, typewritten. The notes were the same.

"Not much to go on there," Annie said. Then she picked up one of the envelopes and examined the postmark. "Wiscasset. Does Cliff know anyone in Wiscasset?"

"He says no." Ian picked up another of the envelopes. "He said they're all posted from Wiscasset. Well, he said all of the ones he *kept* are from Wiscasset."

They inspected the envelopes that the notes had been mailed in. The earliest was postmarked in mid-May and the last was from the previous week and held the forged will. Then they looked at the messages themselves.

"There's just nothing remarkable about these," Annie said at last, exhaling heavily. "Plain type on plain paper in plain envelopes."

"How about the content?" Ian asked, looking them over.

Annie scoffed. "That's plain too. Not particularly well written, not particularly bad. They serve their purpose, I suppose. No big words or strange turns of phrase, no punctuation, all capital letters. They're not threatening. I don't think there's anything criminal about any of them."

"If they could track the guy down, it's possible they could get him for purse snatching, but he didn't steal anything of value, he didn't hurt you, and you didn't see enough to really testify against him. Even if he were convicted, I doubt the penalty would be very severe unless he was a repeat offender."

"All right." Annie frowned at the collection of papers and envelopes spread out over her kitchen table, thinking. "But if he's behind the vandalism and the sabotage at your company, then he ought to be prosecuted for that."

"You're right." There was a flash of anger in Ian's eyes. "Somebody could have gotten hurt in that fire. Whoever did this has an accomplice at the mill too—there have been too many inside jobs. That also would explain how the people who broke the office windows knew when Tim would and wouldn't be making his rounds."

Annie considered for a minute. "Maybe this is oversimplifying things, but do any of your employees live in Wiscasset?"

"Not that I can think of offhand, but I guess it's possible. I can always check our records."

"Why else would all the notes be mailed from Wiscasset? Unless it was especially intended to draw attention from somewhere else. I mean, what in Wiscasset has to do with—" Annie stopped, a slow smile spreading across her face. "Ian, what *is* in Wiscasset?"

"Uh, I don't know."

"The courthouse! I don't know why I didn't think of it before now. That's where I got my purse stolen."

"Do you think that means our purse snatcher lives there? I don't know about that. I mean, he doesn't live at the courthouse or anything."

Annie laughed. "No, but what if the person we want is *working* at the courthouse?"

"What?"

"Remember when we were at the carnival a while ago? And you saw your friend Cliff Bonds there? I don't think I ever mentioned it to you, but while you were putting Petunia in the car for Joanna, I saw the woman from the probate office. When I went to get more records after that, I remembered that I had seen her there. She said she was meeting her boyfriend."

"Boyfriend, eh? I guess that's not unusual."

"Funny that Bonds would be there too, though. And he sure seemed uncomfortable when he was talking to us. In a hurry to get away, you know?" Annie thought for a moment. "Is Bonds married?"

"Yeah, sure." Ian frowned. "Why do you ask?"

"Well, if I remember right, he had two cotton candies that night."

"So maybe one was for his wife."

"Maybe," Annie said. "But if that was the case, why wasn't she with him? And why did he seem so eager to get away from us?"

"I thought that was just because he was mad at me." Ian considered for a moment. "Do you think there's a connection between him and the woman from the probate office? That *he* was the boyfriend she was talking about?"

Annie shrugged. "That might explain how someone knew I had the will and why that same someone was telling Bonds you were taking advantage of him."

"But Bonds got those messages well before you found the will and went to Wiscasset to check into it. How would she know?"

"Maybe she had already done some checking on her own. Checking into what kind of assets the boyfriend had and whether he was worth pursuing."

Ian shook his head. "Cold. Very cold."

"I'd sure like to find out," Annie said. "I'd like to know a lot more about her and this boyfriend of hers, whether it's Bonds or not."

Ian grinned. "Maybe we should just go ask her."

"You don't mind going with me?"

"I insist. Especially after what happened the last time you were at the courthouse."

"I hardly think I'm going to get my purse snatched every time I go to Wiscasset."

"I know, but I'd feel better if I were with you."

She leaned over and put her arms around him. "I'd feel a lot better if you did. The twins have their skit practice again Thursday. Could you get away then?"

"That," Ian said with a smacking kiss, "would be perfect. Now what about anything you might still have here? Any chance there's something up in your attic that might tell us more about the Mayfields? I mean, you found the purse up there."

"No, I don't think so. After I found the will, I went all through that box to see if there was anything else of interest in it. It was just the purse, a couple of dresses and some shoes. And two or three hats too. I think that's all."

Ian considered for a moment. "And you think all that was up in your attic because you and your neighbor played dress-up when you were little with the things Bonnie Thornton Mayfield's mother kept to remember Bonnie by after the accident?"

"Seems the most reasonable explanation, don't you think?"

He nodded. "If that's the case, couldn't there be more at the Thornton house? Letters? A diary? Anything of hers her mother hung on to for sentimental reasons?"

"I don't know. I don't think the Thorntons have lived there for a while. Now it belongs to another family, the Chapmans, and has since before I came back to Stony Point to live."

"Maybe some of Bonnie's things are still up in the attic

of the old Thornton place. Do you think it might be worth asking the Chapmans if you could look around in case there might be something more? Another box of her things? Or maybe something mixed in with some other stuff?"

Annie laughed. "I suppose I could. John's been playing a lot with the Chapman boys, and their mom, Lisa, has been really nice about letting him tag along to baseball games and such. I guess it wouldn't hurt to ask if there was anything left behind by the Thorntons. Hey, maybe we'll get lucky. I'll check with her tomorrow." She slipped her arm through his, giving him a mischievous grin. "When did I ever turn down a chance to find more clues to one of my mysteries?"

*   *   *   *

Lisa Chapman was more than accommodating. While she kept an eye on the twins and her two boys playing in their backyard, she gave Annie free rein up in her attic.

"My husband has some old camping equipment up there," she said, "but besides that and our Christmas things, we don't use it much. There are some old boxes way in the back. I suppose the last owner left them behind, but we haven't gotten around to clearing them out. You're welcome to anything you find back there."

Annie mostly found boxes of old income tax records and check stubs and bills, all of it stretching from the 1950s through the 1990s and all of it belonging to the Thorntons. There were three boxes of toys that appeared to be from the 1930s and '40s, fairly battered but maybe of interest to a collector. There were two boxes of old clothes, some of which Annie was sure must have been Bonnie's. They were much like the dress and purse and other things that had ended up in Gram's attic. In the bottom of one of them was a stack of letters tied up with a faded pink ribbon and a journal.

Annie caught her breath and opened the book. The year was 1920, and in the front was written the name "Bonnie Thornton Mayfield." She snapped it shut and put it back into the box.

"Jackpot."

She put the letters and the journal and the clothes she suspected were Bonnie's all into one box and then carried that box downstairs.

"Find something?" Lisa Chapman asked her.

"I think this box of things might have belonged to Bonnie Mayfield, the woman I've been trying to investigate. Mind if I borrow it for a while?"

Lisa laughed. "You're welcome to keep it. That's just one less thing I'll have to throw out when I finally clean everything out up there."

"Thank you. I appreciate it so much!" Annie turned to the twins. "Come on, now. Tell Mrs. Chapman thank you for letting you come over. We need to go to the library so I can do some more research."

"Do we have to, Grammy?" Joanna asked. "We were right in the middle of follow the leader."

"And they have a cool fort to play in," John said as the two Chapman boys looked at her pleadingly.

"Well, you'll have to play again later," Annie told them. "I'm sure Mrs. Chapman has things she needs to do."

Lisa laughed. "Just my regular housework. You're welcome to leave the twins here if you want. I don't mind keeping an eye on them while they're playing with the boys."

"Please, Grammy?" John begged.

Annie frowned at him, warning him without words to not be a bother, and then she turned again to Lisa. "I really hate to impose."

"It wouldn't be an imposition at all," Lisa said with a laugh. "It would actually be a help to me to have somebody to keep the boys busy while I try to get things done."

Annie laughed too. She knew how that was, for sure. "I'll make it up to you. Next time you have errands to run, you can send the boys over to play. How's that?"

"That would be great, Annie."

Annie gave John and Joanna a stern look. "You two behave yourselves, and mind Mrs. Chapman, do you hear me?"

The twins beamed at her.

"We will!" Joanna said.

"We promise!" John dashed toward the wooden fort in the back corner of the yard. "Thanks, Grammy!"

"You've got my cell number," Annie reminded Lisa, shifting the box against her hip as she walked to the front door. "Give me a call if you need to. I can be back in a flash."

"No hurry." Lisa smiled and waved as Annie walked back toward Grey Gables. "We'll be right here."

*　　*　　*　　*

Deciding that the journal and the letters from the Chapman attic would have to wait until she had more time,

Annie dropped the box off at her kitchen table and then headed over to the Stony Point library to check out the witnesses listed for the 1920 will, Gerald E. Carlson and Elijah Benton.

Then she looked up Carlson and Benton in the 1920 census. But according to the records, they didn't live in Stony Point at that time. Carlson was from Newcastle and Benton lived in Dresden. What could their connection have been to the Butler family? Friends? Neighbors?

Carlson had evidently been a bookkeeper. Annie checked the listing for Benton and realized his occupation was also listed as bookkeeper. That seemed a little strange, unless maybe they had worked at the sawmill. If that were the case, it would have been rather convenient for someone to get them to sign the forged will, and it also would have seemed very natural that Paul Butler would have gotten them to witness his signature while he was at his office.

She'd have to check that out too, if she could. She sighed. She was still getting no closer to figuring this out. The mystery was too old, and there were still too many pieces missing.

She looked at her watch and found it was still only midafternoon, so she called Lisa Chapman to check on the twins. Lisa assured her they were having fun and she need not hurry back, so Annie went back to her research.

She typed "Gerald E. Carlson" into the computer's search engine and got nothing but some genealogical sites confirming the information she already had. Then she put in "Elijah Benton" and got more of the same until something caught her eye toward the bottom of the page:

"... arrested for embezzlement, January 1920; charges dropped, March 1920 ...."

Eyes wide, she clicked the link. There was no detail about the charges beyond what she had already seen in the search results. Evidently this particular genealogist wanted nothing but the unvarnished truth in his records.

Breathless, Annie checked the newspaper archives again, scanning the articles from the date of the forged will until after the Mayfield crash. She'd been all through this once. Surely she couldn't have missed—

Then she saw it: "Charges Dropped in Embezzlement Scandal." The article was from the issue dated March 17, 1920. No wonder she hadn't noticed it. The headline didn't mention the Butlers or the Mayfields.

> *Gerald E. Carlson and Elijah Benton, recently indicted on embezzlement charges brought by their former employer, the late Paul Butler of Butler's Lumber, were released from custody when the firm dropped all charges against them. Robert Mayfield, one of the Butler heirs, told this reporter that he felt the evidence against the pair was circumstantial and that, in light of his grandfather's recent passing, he had no desire to pursue the case. The defendants were not available for comment.*

Annie read through the article about the original indictment and the surrounding circumstances. It was absolute conjecture on her part, of course, but she wondered: *Might Robert Mayfield have dropped the charges against the pair in exchange for their signatures on the forged will?* It made sense, especially since that will would have brought him his grandfather's entire estate. But if so, why had his wife hidden that will? She would have benefited by it too. Or was she perhaps thwarting his plans for another reason?

And what did the mysterious Marlene Bissette of Aunt Minnie's story have to do with all this? How did she fit into the story? Had one of the cousins really been involved with her, and if so, which one? Was she the reason Bonnie Mayfield had hidden the will that would have made her husband wealthy?

Annie went back to her research. There were no Bissettes listed in the 1920 census for Lincoln County. There was no obituary for a Marlene Bissette in the *Chronicle* for 1920 or 1919 or even 1918.

Annie frowned. Maybe Aunt Minnie hadn't remembered the right name. After all, it had been almost eighty years since she had heard that bit of schoolgirl gossip. Funny that she would seem so certain about the name though. So pretty and romantic and tragic, she had said, and she even had that little bit of a verse. Maybe this Marlene hadn't lived in Lincoln County.

Annie went to the computer and, just to see what would come up, typed "Marlene Bissette, Stony Point, Maine" into the search engine. Most of what came up contained only one or two of the words of her search, but one of the ancestry sites listed a Marlene Bissette in Stony Point. Annie held her breath and clicked the link. Then she exhaled heavily. This Marlene Bissette had died in 1871.

Annie read the blurb under the name. Marlene was born in 1852, so she had been only nineteen when she died "under questionable circumstances." Well, that was odd. She had two sisters, and both of them had extensive family connections listed on the site. But poor Marlene was little more than a footnote.

Annie sighed. She didn't have time to get involved with a wild goose chase that had nothing to do with the situation she was investigating. Still that "under questionable circumstances" comment was intriguing. Maybe this *was* the right Marlene, the one Aunt Minnie had heard of—but if she died in 1871, she obviously couldn't have had anything to do with Theo Butler in 1919.

Still, it would be interesting to know what information the 1870 census had on her. Annie checked the Lincoln County records and soon found eighteen-year-old Marlene Bissette listed as working as a maid in Stony Point. Annie's eyes widened. Her name was there below the names of her employer and his family, including his son, Paul Maxwell Butler.

Annie read it over two or three times just to make sure she wasn't mistaken, but there it was in the spidery, faded handwriting of the census taker. Casper Lee Butler, his wife, Irene, and their two sons, Paul Maxwell Butler and Kendrick Lee Butler, had lived in Stony Point in 1870 along with Paul's wife and child and several employees, including their maid, Marlene Bissette. Perhaps this did have something to do with her investigation after all. Maybe Aunt Minnie's story was true, but she had gotten the relationships and dates mixed up. Or maybe the girl who had told her the scandalous story had it all wrong. Either way, they had the wrong era—and the wrong Butlers.

She thought about what Aunt Minnie had said. *The*

old man was raging mad over it. How angry had he been? His son, Paul Butler, had obviously inherited the sawmill and the timberland because he had passed them down to his grandsons. But what had happened to Paul's brother, Kendrick? What had *he* inherited? She'd have to go back to the courthouse and see if she could find whatever will had been probated for Casper Lee Butler. Unless—

She typed the name "Casper Lee Butler" into the computer's search engine along with his date of birth. He was listed on some genealogy sites, but there was no particularly telling information there, just the basics about his ancestors and descendants. She sighed. She'd just have to request a copy of the will when she and Ian went to Wiscasset tomorrow—before they had their little chat with Ms. Burke.

Annie put away the newspaper microfilm and stood up, stretching as she did. A glance at her watch told her she had let the afternoon get away from her. She still didn't have all her questions answered, but at least she had some leads to check out. And she had Bonnie Mayfield's journal to read.

She smiled and went to pick up the twins.

*   *   *   *

"I think I know why Bonnie Mayfield hid the forged will." Annie beamed at Ian as they drove toward Wiscasset the next day. "I wanted to tell you all about it last night after I read her journal, but it was after midnight, and I didn't think you'd appreciate the call."

"Thoughtful of you," he said with a wink. "So what did you find out?"

"Evidently, as your Aunt Minnie said, Robert Mayfield was quite a schemer. Bonnie wrote a lot about how worried she was over his various plans to get rich quick. She wasn't specific in her last few entries, the ones right before the car crash, but she said she and her husband had quite a quarrel about his latest plan. She said, and I quote, 'I'm not going to let him cheat his cousin this way.' It seems pretty clear, don't you think?"

Ian nodded. "I'd say so. She found out about the forged will and slipped it into the lining of her purse to keep it from him. I wonder why she didn't just destroy it. Burn it or something."

"I don't know." Annie shrugged. "Maybe she didn't have time. I'm sure that was what they were quarreling over though, when the accident happened. And all those vague accusations her husband made about foul play in his grandfather's death— those were just to make the forged will look plausible."

"That's too bad." Ian drove in silence for a few minutes, and then he glanced at Annie. "But that still doesn't explain who our little troublemaker is. The will is forged. Cliff Bonds knows now that he doesn't have any right to anything I have. Nobody else stood to gain from that will being valid."

"But Cliff didn't know the will was forged until recently. And there haven't been any incidents since then, have there?"

Ian shook his head. "No. Nothing. I just hate to think Cliff would have done all that. And I hate more than anything to imagine he's got a girlfriend on the side. He's always seemed like a pretty good guy. Not my best friend or anything, but honest at least."

She patted his shoulder. "We don't know for sure about any of this yet. Let's see what our Ms. Burke has to say for herself."

*   *   *   *

Ms. Burke looked up, obviously startled, when Annie and Ian came up to her window.

"Hello," Annie said when the other woman didn't speak. "I'm sure you remember me. I was the one who had her purse stolen a couple of weeks ago."

Ms. Burke smiled faintly. "Yes, of course I remember. Is there something I can do for you?"

"Yes, I need a copy of another will. This time for a Casper Lee Butler."

She filled out the appropriate form, and soon Ms. Burke handed her the requested copy.

"Thank you," Annie said, and then she nodded toward Ian. "This is Ian Butler, the mayor of Stony Point. I don't know if you've heard of him."

Ms. Burke shrugged slightly, her smile polite. "I may have. Is there something else I can help you with today?"

With a glance at Ian, Annie drew a steadying breath. "Is there any reason, Ms. Burke, that you'd have a particular interest in the research I've been doing? A personal interest?"

"I—I don't know what you mean," Ms. Burke sputtered.

Ian raised one eyebrow. "Look, you can tell us what it is, or we can have the police look into it for us. That might not look so good, considering the nature of your job here. Being in a position of trust and everything."

"You were the one who let the purse snatcher into that side door, aren't you?" Annie said.

Annie watched the other woman's eyes. It was only a theory, but it was certainly possible. If she wasn't used to doing this sort of thing, if she had been talked into it or co-erced into it, she might be fairly easy to crack.

She blinked rapidly. "You're not the police."

Ian's lips twitched, and Annie knew he had realized it too. They had her already. If she didn't have something to hide, she wouldn't be so quickly objecting to their lack of authority.

"No, we're not." Ian's voice was grave. "But they're cer-tainly an option."

"You don't have proof of anything, and I don't have to talk to you." Ms. Burke was getting a little red in the face. "If you don't have any real business here, I'm going to have to ask you to leave."

"OK," he said, smiling slightly. "Not a problem. Annie, where did you say the police station is from here?"

Annie looked at the woman, feeling rather sorry for her now. She looked as if she were about to burst into tears.

"You don't really want us to make this an official inves-tigation, do you?" Annie asked, her voice gentle and sym-pathetic. "We don't want to get you into trouble, especially if you're not the one behind all this. We just want to know what's going on."

Ms. Burke put her head in her hands. "It was all my boyfriend's idea."

Annie glanced at Ian and then looked again at Ms. Burke. "His idea and not yours?"

"No, of course it wasn't mine. I've never—" She shook her head. "I've *never* done anything like this. He said it would be OK. I didn't know everything he had in mind."

"You realize he's a married man, don't you?" Ian said, and the woman's eyes widened.

"No. Of course not. He told me he was divorced. He said he had been for a long time." Tears sprang to her eyes. "No."

"Cliff's been married for close to thirty years," Ian told her, his eyes all sympathy.

Ms. Burke blinked hard. "Cliff? Cliff Bonds? I've never even met him. I just mailed the letters. I didn't even know what was in them."

"Cliff isn't your boyfriend?" Annie asked, puzzled. "Then who is?"

The woman dabbed her eyes with a tissue. "His name is Tim."

Ian's eyes flashed. "Wait a minute. You don't mean Tim Butler, do you?"

She nodded miserably.

Annie's mouth dropped open. "Tim Butler who works at the sawmill?"

Again Ms. Burke nodded. "He—he and I have been dating for the past four months."

Annie glanced at Ian. At the carnival, Tim had said he had been seeing his girlfriend for only six weeks. Maybe that was only an excuse to make it seem more reasonable for him not to introduce her.

"He used to come in here all the time to look at wills and deed records," Ms. Burke said. "A lot of the same ones you were looking at. We sort of hit it off, and then we started going out. When I noticed you were looking at a lot of Butler family records, I just happened to mention it to him. He was curious about why you were interested. Of course, I didn't know. I could only tell him which records you had requested. He asked me to make him copies of the same records, which I did. I told him about you asking for a copy of Paul Butler's probated will and that you were comparing it to some other papers you had in your purse."

Ian looked at her, tight-lipped. "So you didn't know what she had in her purse, just that it was likely something to do with Paul Butler."

Ms. Burke turned pleading eyes on him. "I didn't know what he was going to do. He just told me that if she came back and asked for more records, I was supposed to put her off until he could get here. I did. He told me to unlock that side door when she got here, when I went into the back of the office to get the copies she requested. He didn't tell me he was going to steal her purse. I didn't know there was another will."

"So Tim was the purse snatcher."

"Yes." Ms. Burke looked at Annie again. "I didn't know it until he came in through the side door and told me to lock it up behind him. He found the copy of the probated will she had just picked up and the original from 1920. He didn't take anything else, I'm sure of it." She bit her lip. "I'm so sorry about all this."

"But why?" Annie asked Ian. "Why would he care about the wills or the property? What good would it do him to prove the newer one was genuine or not? He's not one of Paul Butler's descendants, is he?"

"No," Ian said. "If I'm remembering right, he's the grandson several times removed of Paul's brother. Unless Paul had made some special provision for his nephew or grandnephew or something, Tim wouldn't have any claim to Paul's property. And what does this have to do with Cliff Bonds? Or does it have anything to do with him at all?"

Ms. Burke could only shrug helplessly. "I just don't know. He hasn't told me anything, and I'm afraid to ask him."

"Afraid?" Annie put one hand on her arm. "He hasn't threatened you or anything, has he?"

The other woman shook her head, looking down at her desk. "I just—I don't want to make him mad. He might not want to see me anymore."

Annie looked over at Ian, not knowing if she wanted to hug the woman or shake some sense into her. "Maybe, Ms. Burke, that's not the worst thing that could happen to you."

She hung her head. "I know it looks awful. But really, he's not a bad guy. He cares about me. He—"

"Just so he could get something he wanted, he talked you into doing something that could get you into a lot of trouble. Trouble with the police and with your job," Ian said, his voice stern. "I guess that says a lot about how much he cares about you."

Ms. Burke glared at him, eyes rimmed in red, but she said nothing, and Ian's expression softened.

"I'm sorry. It just makes me mad to see a man use a lady like that."

She gave him a reluctant, wistful smile. "Too bad there aren't enough good guys to go around."

"Better to not have one at all," Annie said, "than one who doesn't treat you right."

Ms. Burke only frowned slightly. "So I guess you're going to turn me in to the police."

Annie and Ian exchanged a glance. Then Ian nodded slightly at Annie, obviously leaving the decision up to her.

"I don't think we need to go to the police right now," Annie said. "And if we do, we'll try to keep your name out of it if we can. I can't promise you won't have to answer some questions eventually. I just don't know what will happen. Tim might not be too happy once we talk to him."

She sighed heavily. "He'll know I told you, won't he? Even if you don't tell him straight out. He'll have to realize I talked to you."

Annie gave her an understanding smile. "I don't think you have to worry too much. He's going to have trouble enough of his own to deal with."

"You're not afraid of him, are you, Ms. Burke?" Ian's gaze was penetrating. "I wouldn't think he'd hurt anybody, but then again, I wouldn't have thought he'd be behind something like this either."

"No. He never did anything but sweet-talk me." She looked down at the chipped pink polish on her fingernails. "I guess I was just too easily led."

Annie looked at Ian, not sure what she ought to say to the woman. She felt bad for her—she really did—but that didn't make what she had done right.

"Unless there's something else you'd like to tell us," Annie said, "we're leaving now. Thank you for the information. And really, we'll keep you out of this as much as possible."

Ms. Burke nodded, looking resigned to whatever consequences there would be. Annie and Ian walked out to the parking lot.

"So what do you think?" Ian asked. "You're better at reading people than I am. Was she legit?"

"I think so." Annie took his arm, remembering how helpless she had felt when she was in this same parking lot and her purse had been stolen. "Now what do we do?"

"How about taking a look at that will you just got?"

Startled, Annie laughed. "I totally forgot. Let's get back in the car and see."

As Ian drove back to Stony Point, Annie scanned the will until she found the bequests.

I give and bequeath all of my estate, real and personal, or mixed, of which I shall die seized or possessed, to my son Paul Maxwell Butler, including all property which I may acquire or be entitled to after execution of this Will, to be his absolutely, if he survives me, to his use and benefit forever. I have expressly excluded my son Kendrick Lee Butler from any inheritance under the provisions of this Will for matters of conscience.

"Remember that scandalous story your Aunt Minnie told us about Marlene Bissette?" Annie asked.

Ian nodded. "You didn't actually find out something about that, did you? It was true?"

Annie smiled. "Well, yes and no. There was a Marlene Bissette, and evidently she did die under mysterious circumstances. I couldn't find any specifics on that, but she did die very young. And she was one of the maids at the Butler house."

Ian shook his head ruefully. "So she *was* involved with one of the boys. Was it Theo?"

"No. And it wasn't Robert either."

"No?" He gave her a baffled little grin. "So, who?"

"I think it was Kendrick."

"Kendrick from this will? Casper Butler's younger son?"

"Casper Butler must have been the one who disinherited his son, not Paul Butler. And it was because of Marlene Bissette and the scandal surrounding her—a scandal from 1871, not 1920."

"Well, that explains a lot, if it's true," Ian said. "Except it doesn't."

Annie sighed. "I know. It explains why Kendrick was disinherited, but that has nothing to do with Theo. But I guess now you know what happened to Tim's part of the family and why he's working for you instead of having an interest in the mill."

"So Tim's grandfather's Great-Grandfather Kendrick was disinherited, and my grandfather's Great-Grandfather Paul got the mill and the timberland."

Annie nodded. "Which Paul passed down to his grandsons Theo and Robert."

"And Tim's family got nothing." Ian looked faintly disgusted. "So he's been looking over all those deed and probate records for months now, agonizing about how his family has been wronged."

"Seems like," Annie said. "I guess he was just taking his

frustrations out on you and Cliff Bonds until he got hold of that forged will. I suppose by sending that to Bonds, he hoped to really ruin you. It's pretty sad."

"After I tried so hard to help him out." Ian clenched his jaw. "When do you need to pick up the twins?"

Annie checked her watch. "Not for another hour. They're supposed to have some games and snacks after their play practice."

"Good," Ian said. "I think it's time we had a little talk with Tim."

~ 20 ~

*I*an escorted Annie into his office at the sawmill, pulled up a chair for her, and then picked up his phone and punched in an extension.

"Max? Could you find Tim and ask him to come into my office? Great. Thanks."

Ian smiled at Annie when there was a knock on the door. "Here we go."

He got up and let Tim in.

"You wanted to see me, Ian?"

"Sure. Are you busy right now?"

"Just emptying the trash and stuff. What's going on?"

Ian pushed the office door shut. Tim's eyes widened slightly when he saw Annie there.

"You remember Annie Dawson, don't you, Tim?" Ian asked.

Tim managed his usual grin and nodded, extending his hand. "Sure do. How are you, Mrs. Dawson?"

She smiled tautly. "Not very well, Tim. I haven't been since you snatched my purse that day in Wiscasset."

His hand faltered and then dropped back to his side; his pale eyebrows lifted. "Your purse?"

Ian pulled another chair close to the desk. "Why don't you sit down, Tim. I don't think we're going to get this all straightened out in just a few minutes."

Tim shook his head. "I don't know what this is, but I don't think you know what you're talking about. Why would I steal your purse, Mrs. Dawson? What day are you talking about?"

"The nineteenth," Annie said. "I remember because that was what I had to write on the police report."

"The nineteenth?" Tim thought for a moment. "The nineteenth, I was home asleep. I was working nights back then."

"That would give you the perfect opportunity to go down to the courthouse in Wiscasset and wait for me to come out with Paul Butler's will." Annie nodded. "That fits perfectly."

"What will?" Tim looked at Ian. "How would I even know there was a will? And what difference would Paul Butler's will make to me? My part of the family wasn't due anything from him."

Ian crossed his arms over his chest. "So you know who Paul Butler was? That's pretty convenient too."

Tim frowned. "Well, why shouldn't I know the people in my own family?"

"I didn't know who he was," Ian told him. "That's pretty far back to keep track of, isn't it?"

"Well, uh, genealogy is a hobby of mine. There's no harm in that, is there?"

"Depends on what you use it for." Ian put his hands on the back of the empty chair. "I think you should have a seat."

This time Tim took the offer, still looking a little bewildered. "What are you accusing me of?"

"What did you do with the will that was in my purse?" Annie asked.

Tim shook his head. "I don't know how I was supposed to know there was a will in your purse in the first place."

"Maybe you didn't know it was a will, but you knew it was something to do with the Butlers. You knew about the deed records and the probate records I was looking at. You knew I had something in my purse that I was trying to find out more about." Annie pursed her lips. "You've been looking for some way to cause trouble for Ian for a long time, haven't you?"

Again Tim shook his head. "How could I cause him trouble with a will that didn't even have anything to do with my part of the family?"

"Maybe that's the point," she said. "Maybe you resent the fact that Ian owns the sawmill, and you just sweep it up."

Ian looked at her, one eyebrow lifted. Then he looked at his cousin.

"Is that it, Tim? Jealousy? Or is it more than that? How much did you hope to get out of Cliff Bonds by telling him you could get the mill for him? Or were you just trying to mess up our business relationship and stall our contracts?"

Tim frowned, finally dropping the look of hurt and confused innocence. "Fine. Do what you want. I'm not sorry."

"So we guessed right then?" Ian pulled up another chair and straddled it backward, face-to-face with his distant cousin. "You cut the fence, broke the windows, faked the footprints, started the fire, everything. You want to tell us about it?"

"Not so much to tell." Tim shrugged. "You get all the breaks. I don't. Simple as that."

"What's that supposed to mean?"

"Come on, Ian. You're not stupid. Don't act like it. You're the one who got handed this mill on a silver platter. Like the lady says. You own it; I just sweep it up. All you have to do is stand back and rake in the cash."

"Yeah," Ian said drily. "Because there's absolutely no work involved on my part." He laughed, shaking his head, and Tim glared at him.

"It's not fair that Paul Butler inherited everything in the first place. My side of the family should have ended up with something too."

Annie raised one eyebrow. "You've been doing all kinds of research into your family history, Tim. Are you telling me you don't know what happened to Kendrick?"

"It wasn't fair," Tim muttered half under his breath. "Paul practically stole the mill and the timberland from his brother. It wasn't fair, and it wasn't right."

"He ended up with nothing," Annie agreed, "but that wasn't Paul's fault."

"You know what happened, right?" Ian asked again. "About why Kendrick was disinherited?"

Annie glanced at Tim, but he only gave her a sour look.

"It wasn't fair," he insisted. "It wasn't Kendrick's fault that girl killed herself. His father was too hard on him, leaving him with nothing like that. Paul should have given him back half of the mill and the timberland."

Ian shook his head. "Maybe Paul was the one who did all the work while Kendrick played around. Why should he just give Kendrick half of everything when their father didn't think he should have it?"

"Because he was *family*!" Tim glared at Ian. "It wasn't right for him to have his brother working for him the rest of his life. Sweeping up."

"Is that what he did? Worked for Paul?" Annie looked at him dubiously. "For the rest of his life?"

Tim still glared, saying nothing.

"I can find out, you know," Ian said. "In the company records."

Tim made a little huffing sound. "All right, no. He didn't always sweep up. He worked in the office."

"Doing what?" Annie asked.

"I'll look it up," Ian offered when Tim was again silent. "Probably a vice president or something."

"Funny," Tim sneered. "OK, so he was the office manager. Happy? He made all of ninety-eight dollars a month."

Annie's eyebrows went up, but Ian only shook his head.

"Sounds awful. Until you realize most folks back then probably made less than fifty." He smiled at Annie. "I know a little history myself."

"Still isn't right," Tim muttered. "He shouldn't have been working for Paul in the first place. He should have owned at least part of it."

"But he didn't. And that water went under the bridge over a hundred years ago." Ian looked at him for a long moment, considering. "You know, if you spent half the time and effort on something worthwhile that you spend on feeling sorry for yourself, you'd be pretty well off."

"Easy for you to say," Tim spat. "With all the Butler fortune passed down to you."

Ian snorted. "Please. I never heard of any fortune. I certainly never got one passed down to me. Have you ever really checked out how much work it is to run your own business?"

"I wouldn't mind finding out, I can tell you that much—if I could ever get a good start."

Annie gave him a dubious look. "If you really wanted something like that, you would work toward that now."

"I tried it once already." Tim shrugged his shoulders with a sullen frown. "I had my own auto shop, but I couldn't make a go of it. Put a lot of money and time into it too, but I was just … I could never get a decent break. It wasn't fair."

"That's not what Pam said," Ian put in.

Annie looked at him. "Pam?"

"Pam was Tim's wife," Ian said, his eyes on the other man. "I understand you borrowed a lot of money on the house she inherited from her parents and then lost the money and the house because you wouldn't take care of your business when you had it."

"Pam didn't know." Tim's face reddened. "She didn't know how hard it was to get a business going."

"She kept your books, didn't she? She told me you spent all your time hanging out with your friends and souping up their muscle cars for free and never got around to the paying jobs. Eventually you didn't have any paying customers—right?"

Tim crossed his arms over his chest, defiant. "I guess it's different when you have a going business just dumped into your lap. Huh, Ian?"

Ian didn't say anything for a very long time. There was such tension between him and Tim, Annie didn't dare break the silence. Finally, Ian exhaled.

"I want you out of here, Tim. I don't want to see you around the mill or around Stony Point ever again."

Tim's face paled. "But Ian, that's not fair."

"You want fair?" Ian's eyes flashed. "Fair would be me making you pay back every penny your vandalism has cost me—and every penny of lost profits from jobs that didn't get done. Fair would be me reporting you to the police for all your petty little crimes. Fair would be me warning everybody in town never to trust you again. Do you really want fair, Tim?"

Tim shrank back from him. "I—I guess maybe it is time I was moving on."

"Yes. I think that's best," Ian said, cooling a little, and he got up and opened the office door. "You'd better go now. I hope you realize how close you came to being in serious trouble. I hope you never pull anything like this again. You can bet you won't get out of it so easily if you do."

Tim nodded, still wide-eyed.

"Make sure you stop by payroll," Ian added. "You have part of a paycheck coming. I've already let them know you'll be picking it up."

Tim nodded, and without a glance at Annie, slunk out of the office. Ian shut the door again and then collapsed into a chair.

"I guess that's it."

Annie rushed to him, leaning over to put her arms around his neck. "Are you OK?"

"Yeah." He managed a smile. "Glad this is over."

"Me too."

He smiled. They were silent for a moment, and then Annie looked into his eyes.

"Why didn't you turn him over to the police?"

Ian shrugged. "I hope, without an ax to grind, he won't ever do this kind of thing to anyone else. And to be honest, I felt sorry for the lady at the probate office. She's probably never been in trouble her whole life. I didn't want to drag her into all this, and I'm pretty sure she would have been if I'd turned Tim over to the police."

She hugged him close and whispered into his ear, "You're a good man, Ian Butler. Anybody ever tell you that?"

He laughed softly, returning the embrace. "Ma'am, I think you've confused me with someone else."

"That's the second time you've told me that," she said, punctuating it with a kiss. "I'm not confused at all."

*   *   *   *

Annie was exhausted by the time it was time to go to bed. Ian had taken her to pick up the twins from their play practice. On a whim, he had suggested they go ride go-karts, and then they all went swimming in the ocean. Herb and LeeAnn were coming the next day. They'd stay the weekend and then take the twins home. Annie was going to miss her grandchildren. She had known before they came to stay that she would, but now, checking on them before she went to sleep on this last night to have them to herself, she realized just how much.

She tugged the sheet just a little higher up to Joanna's chin and then touched a kiss to her hair. How sweet she looked. How nice it would be to somehow pack this moment into a box in the attic, a box she could take down and look into anytime she liked no matter how the years passed.

Joanna and John would be grown up in the blink of an eye. Annie knew how it was. She had seen it with LeeAnn. It would be the same with the twins.

"Better enjoy it while you can," she murmured, and impulsively, she kissed the sleeping girl once again. "Night-night, sweetie."

She went to the room across the hall. There was enough moonlight for her to see John sitting up in bed staging a fierce battle between his cowboy doll and a plush tiger. When he saw her standing in the doorway, hands on hips, he blinked guiltily.

"Hi, Grammy."

"Which part of bedtime did I not make clear?"

He shrugged. "I guess I'm not tired yet."

"Not tired? And you didn't eat much of your dinner." She sat on the bed and put her arm around him, pulling his head against her shoulder. "What's the matter, honey? You haven't seemed like you've had a good time here on this trip."

That little bit of hardness she had seen before came into his expression, and he pulled away from her. "Nothing. I probably should go to sleep now."

"John." She put one finger under his chin and turned his face up to her. "I thought you and I always talked about things. Is there something you want to tell me?"

His lower lip quivered, and then he frowned, face hard once again. "Are you going to marry Mr. Ian?"

That startled a low laugh out of her. "I—I don't know, honey. That's something we'll have to see about later on. Right now, he and I are just seeing if we might be right for each other. Don't you like Mr. Ian? You used to, I know."

John shrugged, still having that hardness in his little face. "I guess he's OK."

"But?"

He sighed and then snuggled against her. "Don't you love *us* anymore, Grammy?"

"Oh, John." She hugged him as tightly as she possibly could and then kissed the top of his head. "Of *course* I do. Why would you even ask that?"

"Then what do you want him for?"

She toyed with the strands of fair hair at the nape of his neck. "You know, your grandpa and I loved each other very much, the special kind of way your mom and dad love each other. You didn't mind that, did you?"

"No," he said after a long moment's thought. "But that was different. He was … Grandpa."

"But just because I loved him didn't mean I didn't love you and Joanna, did it?"

He frowned and shrugged, reluctantly conceding the point.

She kissed him again. "Just because I grow to love someone new doesn't mean I can't keep loving you too. Love isn't like a pie or a meat loaf where you can run out if you give too many people a piece. Love just keeps getting bigger and bigger the more people you give it to."

He didn't say anything.

"Besides," she added finally, "you're going to be going home in a couple of days. I'll be up here all by myself. You wouldn't want me to be all alone, would you?"

The frown turned into a pout. "Guess not."

She smiled a little, snuggling him closer. "And come on,

admit it, Mr. Ian's a pretty good guy, isn't he? I mean, he did let you beat him in a sword fight and everything, right?"

John giggled. "He was pretty funny."

"He was, wasn't he?"

John was quiet again, and then he sighed. "But *are* you going to marry him, Grammy?"

"I just don't know yet, honey. Getting married is a very serious thing to do, and you should be pretty sure before you decide to do it."

He nodded wisely. "'Cause then you're stuck, right?"

She stifled a laugh. "Well, it's not a decision you should make without thinking about it very, very hard. After all, when you get married, you promise to love that person as long as you are both alive, so you ought to be pretty sure that's really what you want to do."

He put one arm around her and snuggled closer. "Grammy, would it make you happy to have somebody special like Grandpa was?"

"It's always nice to have somebody special, honey. We'll just have to wait and see if Mr. Ian is the special one for me." She squeezed him tightly. "And even if he is, that doesn't mean we forget about Grandpa."

John nodded against her. "Good."

A tremendous yawn caught him by surprise, and Annie smiled at him.

"I think it's time you stopped worrying about what might happen and get some sleep."

She laid him back on his pillow, and he wriggled down into the covers, tucking his tiger and his cowboy in next to him.

"Do you think Mr. Ian would like to be our grandpa?"

"Well, let me see." She pulled the sheet up to his chin and then tapped one finger on his nose. "He plays games with you. And he brings you treats. And he takes you to the beach and to the park and to the carnival and to drive go-karts. And he carries you when you're tired. And he tells you stories. And he lets you tell him stories. Hmmm ... what do you think?"

There was a grin on John's face now, even if it was a sleepy one.

"I guess that would be OK. As long as you still love us too."

"Always. And maybe you should tell Mr. Ian you're not mad at him next time you see him, huh?"

"Yeah."

She kissed his forehead. "Now, close your eyes and have sweet dreams. Did you say your prayers?"

He nodded.

"All right then. Good night. And don't worry. Whatever happens between Mr. Ian and me doesn't mean anything will be different between you and me. All right, sweetie?"

"OK." He closed his eyes. "Good night, Grammy. I love you."

"I love you too."

*   *   *   *

"Are you ready for this?" Annie asked Ian as they stood on Grey Gables's front porch waiting for Herb and LeeAnn to arrive.

He gave her a sheepish grin. "As I'll ever be, I suppose."

She put her arm around his waist and gave him a one-armed hug. "You have nothing to worry about. You've met them before and lived to tell the tale."

"I know, but things have changed since then."

"It'll be all right," she assured him. "It's not like you'll be asking my father if you may court me. They know we're dating. It's not like we have some big announcement to make or anything."

"I don't know. Sometimes I think grown children can be a lot tougher than parents ever were."

She giggled. "At least this one is my grown child and not yours."

Laughing, he turned her to face him and wrapped her in his arms. He gave her a quick kiss on the nose and then looked into her eyes, suddenly serious.

"You don't really think they'll mind, do you? I mean, if we're serious?"

"Herb won't mind. In fact, I get the idea that he's known it for a little while now." She shrugged. "On the other hand, LeeAnn was always her daddy's little girl. It's nothing to do with you, I'm sure. She likes you a lot, in fact. She's told me so more than once. But the idea of me getting serious about someone ... Well it's not something she's completely come to grips with yet. We'll just have to give her time to get used to it."

She nestled closer to him and was surprised when he pulled back from her a little.

"I don't think LeeAnn's the only one who needs a little time to get used to the idea."

Ian nodded toward the door behind her, and Annie turned to see John standing there, his little forehead wrinkled in thought.

"Hello, John," she said, smiling. "Did you come to talk to Mr. Ian?"

John looked rather uncertain, and then he gave her a reluctant nod. "If it's OK."

Ian got down on one knee, putting himself nearer to eye level with John. "What would you like to talk about, little man?"

The boy glanced at Annie and then turned back to Ian. "I didn't want you to think I was mad at you. I'm really not."

Ian smiled. "I wouldn't want you to be. And I'm glad you're not."

John hesitated again. "I was … um … wondering if you, uh, if you and Grammy were still deciding if you like each other."

"Oh, we decided that a long time ago," Ian told him. "We like each other a lot. Is that OK with you?"

John shrugged. "Guess so."

"I'm not going to take your grammy away from you, John. I wouldn't want to, and more importantly, your grammy would never let me." Ian looked at him steadily. "She told me you and your sister are very special to her, and that she wouldn't want anything to get in the way of that."

A little bit of a grin tugged at John's mouth. "She did?"

"She did. Pretty cool, huh?"

John only shrugged again, but the grin didn't go away. "Mr. Ian?"

"Yes?"

"Do you—" John bit his lip. "Would you like to be our grandpa? You can think about it for a while if you want to."

"Now that's one thing I don't have to think about at all. I'd like that very, very much. In fact, even if Grammy and I just stay friends like we are now and nothing more, I'd still like to be really good friends with you and Joanna too. What do you think? Would you like that?"

"Could we still go to carnivals and stuff?"

Ian nodded. "Absolutely. What do you say?"

John considered for a moment. "And we could have sword fights too?"

"Oh, yeah, we have to have sword fights, because I'm going to beat you one day. You just wait and see."

John giggled. "You can't beat me. King Miraz never beats High King Peter. Didn't you know that?"

"I suppose you're right." Ian sighed dramatically. "Oh well, I guess that's the way it has to be."

"You know what?" John asked, his voice low and conspiratorial. "Maybe sometimes you can be Peter."

"I used to be a pretty good High King, you know." Ian winked at him. "And maybe sometimes you can be wicked old King Miraz. He's pretty fun too."

John giggled again. "Yeah, that'd be fun."

Annie smiled, watching them, and then she turned, hearing the sound of a car pulling into the driveway.

"Look who's here!" She opened the front door and leaned inside. "Joanna, hurry up! Mommy and Daddy are here!" She heard a shrill squeal from upstairs. "And don't run on the stairs!"

Before Herb and LeeAnn could get out of their car,

Joanna was down the stairs and through the front door. She and John ran, whooping, to their parents.

"Mama! Daddy!"

The twins were immediately scooped up, John in his mother's arms and Joanna in her father's. After hugs and a couple of sound kisses, they switched off. Herb finally put John back on his feet.

"What are they feeding you up here, boy? You're going to be ten feet tall by next month."

Joanna leaned out of LeeAnn's arms and hugged her father's neck. "Did I grow, Daddy? Did I grow too?"

"You sure did, sweetie. I guess some boy is going to want to run away with you before long."

"Eww, no!"

He kissed her cheek and hugged her tightly again. "Darn right. No boys till you're at least forty."

Annie and LeeAnn laughed, and so did Ian as he came down the porch steps.

"Good to see you both." He shook Herb's hand. "Did you have a good drive up?"

"We did." Herb smiled at his wife. "Got a chance to do a lot of talking and figuring things out. And we got a lot of peace and quiet for once." He jostled Joanna in his arms. "Now we're ready to open the zoo again."

"Daddy!" she protested, giggling.

"Are we going to the zoo?" John asked. "You said we could go when we drive through St. Louis. Can we?"

"All right, buddy, we will."

LeeAnn took John's hand. "If we have time. Right now, we're going to eat lunch."

Ian smiled. "I think maybe I should take off now and let you have some family time. I'm sure you're ready to relax for a while after the drive."

"Actually, we've been taking it pretty easy," LeeAnn told him. "We stayed in Portland last night, so we only had to make about sixty miles before lunch."

"Yeah, it hasn't been bad," Herb said. "We're going to take our time going home too. I decided to take it easy for a while."

Annie glanced at LeeAnn and then at Herb. "And then?"

Herb shrugged. "I'm going to stay at my job, unless a better job comes along. When I'm an old man, I don't want to end up regretting not spending time with my family instead of killing myself trying to get ahead."

LeeAnn slipped her arm through his. "And we'd much rather have your time than your money."

"I don't think you'll be sorry," Annie said, glad to see they had worked out their situation. "I think we should all spend as much time as we can with the people we love."

Mirroring her daughter, Annie took Ian's arm. "And I think you ought to stay for lunch with us, Ian. You might as well get to know my family a little better."

LeeAnn frowned slightly. "Now?"

John put his hands on his hips. "Mr. Ian likes Grammy, and Grammy likes Mr. Ian." He sighed heavily. "And I guess it's OK."

"Likes as in just-dating-the-way-you-already-were likes, Mom? Or likes as in headed-toward-something-more-serious likes?" LeeAnn blinked at her mother.

Annie tried to tone down her smile, but she knew her

eyes were shining. "I've thought about it a long time. Just ask Ian."

Ian laughed and nodded. "A long, *long* time."

Annie laughed. "Let's just say we're pretty comfortable where we are right now, and we are thinking about where we might want to end up."

Herb grinned at LeeAnn. "That's OK, isn't it, honey?"

LeeAnn gave her mother a reluctant smile. "Well, if John says it's OK, I guess it is."

Her arm still through Ian's, Annie reached her free hand out to her daughter, caressing her cheek.

"Let's all go inside, grab some lunch, and get caught up."